CW00647220

Come Out of the Kitchen!

A Romance

Alice Duer Miller

Come Out of the Kitchen! A Romance

The present edition is a reproduction of previous publication of this classic work. Minor typographical errors may have been corrected without note; however, for an authentic reading experience the spelling, punctuation, and capitalization have been retained from the original text.

ISBN: 978-1-64799-785-4

CONTENTS

I

THE window of Randolph Reed's office was almost completely covered by magnificent gold block lettering. This to any one who had time and ability to read it—and the former was more common in the community than the latter—conveyed the information that Reed dealt in every kind of real estate, from country palaces to city flats. The last item was put in more for the sake of symmetry than accuracy, for the small Southern town contained nothing approaching an apartment house.

From behind this pattern of gold, Reed peered eagerly one autumn afternoon, chewing the end of a frayed cigar, and listening for the sound of a motor. He was a stout young man, of an amiable though unreadable countenance, but like many people of a heavy build, he was capable of extreme quickness of movement. This was never more clearly shown than when, about four o'clock, the wished for sound actually reached his ears. A motor was approaching.

With a bound Reed left the window, and, seated at his desk, presented in the twinkling of an eye the appearance of a young American business man, calm and efficient, on an afternoon of unusual business pressure. He laid papers in piles, put them in clips and took them out, snapped rubber bands about them with frenzied haste, and finally seizing a pen, he began to indite those well-known and thrilling words: "Dear Sir: Yours of the 15th instant received and contents—" when the motor drew up before his door.

It was an English car; all green and nickel; it moved like an expert skater on perfect ice. As it stopped, the chauffeur dropped from his place beside the driver. The driver himself, removing his glasses, sprang from the car and up the office steps, slapping the pockets of his coat as he did so in a search which soon appeared to be for cigarettes and matches.

"Sorry to be late," he said.

Reed, who had looked up as one who did not at once remember, in his vast preoccupation, either his visitor or his business, now seemed to recall everything. He waved the newcomer to a chair, with a splendid gesture.

"Doubtless the roads," he began.

"Roads!" said the other. "Mud-holes. No, we left Washington later than I intended. Well, have you got the house for me?"

Reed offered his client a cigar.

"No, thank you, prefer my cigarette if you don't mind."

Reed did not mind in the least. The real estate business in Vestalia was never brilliant, and several weeks' profits might easily have been expended in one friendly smoke.

His client was a man under thirty, of a type that used to be considered typically American—that is to say, Anglo-Saxon, modified by a century or so of New England climate and conscience. His ancestors had been sailors, perhaps, and years of exposure had tanned their skins and left their eyes as blue as ever. His movements had the gentleness characteristic of men who are much with horses, and though he was active and rather lightly built, he never was sudden or jerky in any gesture. Something of this same quietness might be detected in his mental attitude. People sometimes thought him hesitating or undecided on questions about which his mind was irrevocably made up. He took a certain friendly interest in life as a whole, and would listen with such patience to an expression of opinion that the expresser of it was often surprised to find the opinion had had no weight with him, whatsoever.

He stood now, listening with the politest attention to Reed's somewhat flowery description of the charms of the Revelly house—charms which Crane himself had examined in the minutest detail.

"Never before," exclaimed the real estate agent, in a magnificent peroration, "never before has the splendid mansion been rented—"

"Ah," said Crane with a smile, "I believe you there."

"Never been offered for rent," corrected the real estate agent, with a cough. "Its delightful colonial flavor—"

"Its confounded dilapidation," said the prospective tenant.

"Its boxwood garden, its splendid lawns, its stables, accommodating twenty-five horses—"

"Yes, if they don't lean up against the sides."

Reed frowned.

"If," he remarked with a touch of pride, "you do not want the house—"

The young man of the motor car laughed good-temperedly.

"I thought we had settled all that last week," he said. "I do want the house; I do appreciate its beauties; I do not consider it in good repair, and I continue to think that the price for six weeks is very high. Have the owners come down?"

Reed frowned again.

"I thought I made it clear, on my part," he answered, "that Mr. and Mrs. Revelly are beyond the reach of communication. They are on their way to Madeira. Before they left they set the price on their house, and I can only follow their instructions. Their children—there are four children—"

"Good heavens, I don't have to rent them with the house, do I?" exclaimed the other frivolously.

The real estate agent colored, probably from annoyance.

"No, Mr. Crane," he answered proudly, "you do not, as far as I know, have to do anything you do not wish to do. What I was about to say was that the children have no authority to alter the price determined by their parents. To my mind, however, it is not a question of absolute value. There is no doubt that you can find newer and more conveniently appointed houses in the hunting district—certainly cheaper ones, if price be such an object. But the Revelly family—one of the most aristocratic families south of Mason and Dixon's, sir—would not be induced to consider renting under the sum originally named."

"It's pretty steep," said the young man, but his mild tone already betrayed him. "And how about servants?"

"Ah," said Reed, looking particularly mask-like, "servants! That has been the great difficulty. To guarantee domestic service that will satisfy your difficult Northern standards—"

"I am fussy about only two things," said Crane, "cooking and boots. Must have my boots properly done."

"If you could have brought your own valet—"

"But I told you he has typhoid fever. Now, see here, Mr. Reed, there really isn't any use wasting my time and yours. If you have not been able to get me a staff of servants with the house, I wouldn't dream of taking it. I thought we had made that clear."

Reed waved his impatient client again to his chair.

"There are at this moment four well-recommended servants yonder in the back office, waiting to be interviewed."

"By me?" exclaimed Crane, looking slightly alarmed.

Reed bowed.

"I wish first, however," he went on, "to say a word or two about them. I obtained them with the greatest difficulty, from the Crosslett-Billingtons, of whom you have doubtless often heard."

"Never in my life," said Crane.

Reed raised his eyebrows.

"He is one of our most distinguished citizens. His collection of tapestry, his villa at Capri—Ah, well, but that is immaterial! The family is now abroad, and has in consequence consented, as a personal favor to me, to allow you to take over four of their servants for the six weeks you will be here, but not a minute longer."

Crane leaned back and blew smoke in the air.

"Are they any good?" he asked.

"You must judge for yourself."

"No, you must tell me."

"The butler is a competent person; the skill of the cook is a proverb—but we had better have them come in and speak to you themselves."

"No, by Jove!" cried Crane, springing to his feet. "I don't think I could stand that." And he incontinently rushed from the office to the motor, where three mummy-like figures on the back seat had remained immovable during his absence.

Of these, two were female and one male. To the elder of the women, Crane applied, hat in hand.

"Won't you give me the benefit of your advice, Mrs. Falkener," he said. "The agent has some servants for me. The wages and everything like that have all been arranged, but would you mind just looking them over for me and telling me what you think about them?"

To invite Mrs. Falkener to give her advice on a detail of household management was like inviting a duck to the pond. She stepped with a queen-like dignity from the car. She was a commanding woman who swam through life, borne up by her belief in her own infallibility. To be just, she was very nearly infallible in matters of comfort and domestic arrangement, and it was now many years since she had given attention to anything else in the world. She was a thorough, able and awe-inspiring woman of fifty-three.

Now she moved into Reed's office, with motor-veils and dusters floating about her, like a solid wingless victory, and sat down in Randolph Reed's own chair. (It was part of her philosophy never to interview a social inferior until she herself was seated.) With a slight gesture of her gloved hand, she indicated that the servants might be admitted to her presence.

The door to the back office opened and the four candidates entered. The first was the butler, a man slightly younger in years than most of those careworn functionaries. He came forward with a quick, rapid step, turning his feet out and walking on his toes. Only Mrs. Falkener recognized that it was the walk of a perfect butler. She would have engaged him on the spot, but when she noted that his hair was parted from forehead back to the line of his collar and brushed slightly forward in front of his ears, she experienced a feeling of envy and for the first time thought with dissatisfaction of the paragon she had left in charge of her own pantry at home.

She did indeed ask him a question or two, just to assure herself of his English intonation, which, it must be owned, a residence in the South had slightly influenced. And then with a start she passed on to the next figure—the cook.

On her the eyes of her future employer had already been fixed since the door first opened, and it would be hardly possible to exaggerate the effect produced by her appearance. She might have stepped from a Mid-Victorian Keepsake, or Book of Beauty. She should have worn eternally a crinoline and a wreath of flowers; her soft gray-blue eyes, her little bowed mouth, her slim throat, should have been the subject of a perpetual steel engraving. She was small, and light of bone, and her hands, crossed upon her check apron (for she was in her working dress), were so little and soft that they seemed hardly capable of lifting a pot or kettle.

Mrs. Falkener expressed the general sentiment exactly when she gasped:

"And you are the cook?"

The cook, whose eyes had been decorously fixed upon the floor, now raised them, and sweeping one rapid glance across both her employer and the speaker, whispered discreetly:

"Yes, ma'am."

"What is your name?"

And at this question a curious thing happened. The butler and Reed answered simultaneously. Only, the butler said "Jane," and Reed, with equal conviction, said "Ellen."

Ignoring this seeming contradiction, the cook fixed her dove-like glance on Mrs. Falkener and answered:

"My name is Jane-Ellen, ma'am."

It was impossible for even as conscientious a housekeeper as Mrs. Falkener to be really severe with so gentle a creature, but she contrived to say, with a certain sternness:

"I should like to see your references, Jane-Ellen."

"Oh, I'm sure that will be all right, Mrs. Falkener," said Crane hastily. He had never removed his eyes from the face of his future cook.

But Jane-Ellen, with soft gestures of those ridiculous hands, was already unfolding a paper, and now handed it to Mrs. Falkener.

That lady took it and held it off at arm's length while she read it.

"And who," she asked, turning to Reed, "is this Claudia Revelly? Mrs. Revelly, I suppose?"

"Why, no," answered Reed. "No, as I told you, Mrs. Revelly is in Madeira with her husband. This is one of the Miss Revellys."

"Humph," replied Mrs. Falkener. "It is a flattering reference, but in my time the word 'recommend' was spelled with only one 'c.'"

The cook colored slightly and flashed a glance that might have been interpreted as reproachful at Reed, who said hastily:

"Ah, yes, quite so. You know—the fact is—our Southern aristocracy—the Revellys are among our very—However, there can be no question whatever about Jane-Ellen's ability. You will, I can assure you from personal experience, be satisfied with her cooking. Mrs. Crosslett-Billington—"

"Humph!" said Mrs. Falkener again, as one who does not mean to commit herself. "We shall see. Let the housemaid come a little forward."

At this a young woman advanced; she bore a certain resemblance of feature to the butler, but entirely lacked his competent alertness.

"This young woman looks to me sullen," Mrs. Falkener observed to Crane, hardly modulating her clear, dry tone of voice.

Crane betrayed his embarrassment. He wished now that he had not invited his elderly friend's coöperation.

"Oh," he said, "I'm sure it will be all right. It must be a trifle annoying to be looked over like this."

"The best way to settle this sort of thing is at the start," replied Mrs. Falkener, and turning to the housemaid, she asked her her name.

"Lily," replied the young woman, in a deep voice of annoyance.

"Lily," said Mrs. Falkener, as if this were a most unsuitable name for a housemaid, and she looked up at Crane to confirm her opinion, but he was again looking at the cook and did not notice her.

"Well, Lily," continued the elder lady, as if she made a distinct concession in making use of such a name at all in addressing a servant, "do you or do you not want to take this place? There is, I suppose, nothing to compel you to take it if you do not want. But now is the time to say so."

Lily, with a manner that did seem a little ungracious, replied that she did want it, and added, on receiving a quick glance from the butler, Smithfield, "Madame."

"Well, then," said Mrs. Falkener, becoming more condescending, "we shall expect a more pleasant demeanor from you, a spirit of coöperation. Nothing is more trying for yourself or your fellow servants—"

Reed moved forward and whispered in Mrs. Falkener's ear:

"It will straighten out of itself, my dear madame—nothing but a little embarrassment—a grande dame like yourself, you understand me, a tremendous impression on a young woman of this sort—"

Mrs. Falkener interrupted him.

"What is the name of the boy in the corner?" she asked.

At this, a round-faced lad of perhaps eighteen sprang forward. The most striking items of his costume were a red neckerchief and a green baize apron and leggings, giving to his appearance a slight flavor of a horse-boy in an illustration to Dickens.

"I, ma'am," he said, with a strong cockney accent, "am the Useful Boy, as they say in the States."

"He's very good at doing boots," said Reed.

"Boots," cried the boy, and kissing his hand he waved it in the air with a gesture we have been accustomed to think of as continental rather than British, "a boot, particularly a riding-boot, is to me—"

"What is your name?" Mrs. Falkener asked, and this time the severity of her manner was unmistakable.

It did not, however, dampen the enthusiasm of the last candidate.

"My name, ma'am," he replied, "is B-r-i-n-d-l-e-b-u-r-y."

"Brindlebury?"

"Pronounced, 'Brinber'—the old Sussex name with which, ma'am, I have no doubt you, as a student of history—"

Mrs. Falkener turned to Crane.

"I think you will have trouble with that boy," she said. "He is inclined to be impertinent."

Crane looked at the boy over her head, and the boy, out of a pair of twinkling gray eyes, looked back. They both managed to look away again before a smile had been actually exchanged, but Crane found himself making use for the third time of his favorite formula:

"Oh, I think I'll find him all right."

Mrs. Falkener, remembering the pitiable weakness of men, again waved her hand.

"They may go now," she said to Reed, who hastily shepherded the four back again into the back office. When they were alone, she turned to Crane and said with the utmost conviction:

"My dear Burton, none of those servants will do—except the butler, who appears to be a thoroughly competent person. But those young women—they may have been anything. Did you not observe that their nails had been manicured?"

Crane stammered slightly, for the fact had not escaped him, in connection, at least, with one of the young women.

"Don't—don't cooks ever manicure their nails?" he said. "It seems rather a good idea to me."

Reed, who was once more approaching, caught these last words.

"Ah," he said, "you were speaking of the manicuring of servants' nails—"

Mrs. Falkener gave him a severe look.

"I was advising Mr. Crane not to engage any one but the butler."

"Indeed, how very interesting," said Reed. "Your judgment in the matter is very valuable, madame, I know, but perhaps you do not sufficiently emphasize the difficulties of getting any servants at all in this part of the country. In fact, I could not undertake, if these are not engaged—"

"Well, I could," said the lady. "I could telegraph to New York to my own intelligence office and have three really competent people here by to-morrow evening."

For a moment Reed looked profoundly distressed, and then he went on:

"Exactly, I have no doubt, madame. But what I was about to say was that I could not undertake to rent the Revelly house to a staff of unknown Northern servants. You see, these two young women have been practically brought up in the household of Mrs. Crosslett-Billington—an old family friend of the Revellys—and they know they would take care of things in the way they are accustomed to—"

"Of course, of course, very natural," said Crane. "I quite agree. I'm willing to give these people a chance. Of course, Mrs. Falkener, I don't know as much about these things as you do, but it's only for a few weeks, and as for their nails—"

"Oh, I can explain that," cried Reed; "in fact, I should have done so at the start. It's an idiosyncrasy of Mr. Billington's. He insists that all the servants in the house should be manicured, particularly those who wait on table, or have anything to do with touching the food."

Mrs. Falkener compressed her lips till they were nothing but a seam in her face.

"Humph!" she said again, and without another word she turned and swept out of the office.

Left alone, the two men stood silent, without even looking at each other, and finally it was Crane who observed mildly:

"Well, you know, they are a little queer in some ways—"

"Take my word for it," said Reed, earnestly, "you will make no mistake in engaging them all—except that boy, but you can manage him, I have no doubt. As for the cook, you will be surprised. Her cooking is famous in three counties, I assure you."

An instant later, the lease was duly signed.

When the motor was safely on its way back to Washington, Mrs. Falkener gave her companions on the back seat the benefit of her own impression. One was her daughter, a muscular, dark-eyed girl, who imagined that she had thoroughly emancipated herself from her mother's dominance because she had established a different field of interest. She loved out-of-door sport of all kinds, particularly hunting, and was as keen and competent about them as her mother was about household management. The two respected each other's abilities, and managed to lead an affectionate life in common.

The man on the back seat was Solon Tucker—Crane's lawyer, by inheritance rather than by choice. He was a thin, erect man, with a narrow head and that expression of mouth at once hard and subtle that the Law writes on so many men's faces. His mind was excellently clear, his manner reserved, and his invariable presupposition that all human beings except himself were likely to make fools of themselves. He had, however, immense respect for Mrs. Falkener's opinions on any subject except law—on which he respected nobody's opinions but his own, least of all those of judges; and he believed that nothing would so effectively lighten his own responsibilities in regard to Crane as to marry him to Mrs. Falkener's daughter, an idea in which Mrs. Falkener cordially agreed.

"You must make a point of staying with him, Solon," she was now murmuring into that gentleman's rather large ear, "if, as I fear, he actually takes this house. You have never seen such an extraordinary group of servants—except the butler. Do you suppose it could be a plot, a blackmailing scheme of some sort? The cook—Well, my dear Solon, a pocket Venus, a stage ingénue, with manicured nails! He was determined to engage her from the first. It seems very unsafe to me. A bachelor of Burton's means. You must stay by him, Solon. In fact," she added, "I think we had better both stay by him. Poor boy, he has no idea of taking care of himself."

"He can be very obstinate," said his lawyer. "But I fancy you exaggerate the dangers. You are unaccustomed to any but the very highest type of English servant. They are probably nothing worse than incompetent."

"Wait till you see the cook!" answered Mrs. Falkener portentously.

Tucker looked away over the darkening landscape.

"Dear me," he thought to himself. "What a mountain she makes of a mole-hill! How every one exaggerates—except trained minds!"

In Tucker's opinion all trained minds were legal.

II

ON the following Monday, late in the afternoon, the old Revelly house was awaiting its new master. Already hunters, ponies, two-wheeled carts, an extra motor, to say nothing of grooms, stable-boys, and a tremendous head coachman, had arrived and were making the stable yards resound as they had not done for seventy years. But they had nothing to do with the household staff. They were all to be boarded by the coachman's wife who was installed in the gardener's cottage.

The house, with its tall pillared portico and flat roofed wings, lost its shabby air as the afternoon light grew dimmer, and by six o'clock, when Crane's motor drew up before the door, it presented nothing but a dignified and spacious mass to his admiring eyes.

No one but Tucker was with him. He had had some difficulty in avoiding the pressing desire of the two Falkener ladies to be with him at the start and help him, as they put it, "get everything in order." He had displayed, however, a firmness that they had not expected. He had been more embarrassed than he cared to remember by Mrs. Falkener's assistance in the real estate office, and he decided to begin his new housekeeping without her advice. He would, indeed, have dispensed with the companionship even of Tucker for a day or two, but that would have been impossible without a direct refusal, and Burton was unwilling to hurt the feelings of so true and loyal a friend, not only of his own but of his father before him.

The dignified butler and the irrepressible boy, Brindlebury, ran down the steps to meet them, and certainly they had no reason to complain of their treatment; bags were carried up and unstrapped, baths drawn, clothes laid out with the most praiseworthy promptness.

Tucker had advocated a preliminary tour of inspection.

"It is most important," he murmured to Crane, "to give these people the idea from the start that you cannot be deceived or imposed upon." But Crane refused even to consider such questions until he had had a bath and dinner.

The plan of the old house was very simple. On the right of the front door was the drawing-room, on the left a small library and a room which had evidently been used as an office. The stairs went up in the center, shallow and broad, winding about a square well. The dining-room ran across the back of the house.

When Tucker came down dressed for dinner, he found Crane was ahead of him. He was standing in the drawing-room bending so intently over something on a table that Tucker, who was not entirely without curiosity, came and bent over it, too, and even the butler, who had come to announce dinner, craned his neck in that direction.

It was a miniature, set in an old-fashioned frame of gold and pearls. It represented a young woman in a mauve tulle ball dress, full in the skirt and cut off the shoulders, as was the fashion in the days before the war. She wore a wreath of fuchsias, one of which trailing down just touched her bare shoulder.

"Well," said Tucker contemptuously, "you don't consider that a work of art, do you?"

Burton remained as one entranced.

"It reminds me of some one I know," he answered.

"It is quite obviously a fancy picture," replied Tucker, who was something of a connoisseur. "Look at those upturned eyes, and that hand. Did you ever see a live woman with such a tiny hand?"

"Yes, once," said Crane, but his guest did not notice him.

"The sentimentality of the art of that period," Tucker continued, "which is so plainly manifested in the poetry——"

"Beg pardon, sir," said Smithfield, "the soup is served."

Crane reluctantly tore himself from the picture and sat down at table, and such is the materialism of our day that he was evidently immediately compensated.

"By Jove," he said, "what a capital purée!"

Even Tucker, who, under Mrs. Falkener's tuition, had intended to find the food uneatable, was obliged to confess its merits.

"I say," said Crane to Smithfield, "tell the cook, will you, that I never tasted such a soup—not out of Paris, or even in it."

"She probably never heard of Paris," put in Tucker.

Smithfield bowed.

"I will explain your meaning to her, sir," he said.

Dinner continued on the same high plane, ending with two perfect cups of coffee, which called forth such eulogies from Crane that Tucker said finally, as they left the dining-room:

"Upon my word, Burt, I never knew you cared so much about eating."

"I love art, Tuck," said the other, slapping his friend on the back. "I appreciate perfection. I worship genius."

Tucker began to feel sincerely distressed. Indeed he lay awake for hours, worrying. He had counted, from Mrs. Falkener's description, on finding the servants so incompetent that the house would be impossible. He had hoped that one dinner would have been enough to send Crane to the telegraph office of his own accord, summoning servants from the North. He had almost promised Mrs. Falkener that when she and her daughter arrived the next afternoon, they would find a new staff expected, if not actually installed. Instead he would have to greet her with the news that the pocket Venus with the polished nails had turned out to be a cordon bleu. That is, if she were really doing the cooking. Perhaps—this idea occurred to Tucker shortly before dawn—perhaps she was just pretending to cook; perhaps she had hired some excellent old black Mammy to do the real work. That should be easily discoverable.

He determined to learn the truth; and on this resolution fell asleep.

The consequence was that he came down to breakfast rather cross, and wouldn't even answer Crane, who was in the most genial temper, when he commented favorably on the omelette. In fact, he let it appear that this constant preoccupation with material details was distasteful to him.

Crane, as he rose from the table, turned to Smithfield:

"Will you tell the cook I'd like to see her," he said. "I'm expecting some ladies to stay, this afternoon, and I want to make things comfortable for them. Be off, Tuck, there's a good fellow, if this sort of thing bores you."

But wild horses would not at that moment have dragged Tucker away, and he observed that he supposed there was no objection to his finishing his breakfast where he was.

Smithfield coughed.

"I'm sure I beg your pardon, sir," he said, "but if you could tell me what it is you want, I would tell the cook. She has a peculiar nature, Jane-Ellen has, sir; has had from a child; and, if you would forgive the liberty, I believe it would be best for you not to interview her yourself."

Tucker looked up quickly.

"Why, what do you mean?" asked Crane.

"She is very timid, sir, very easily affected by criticism—"

"Good heavens, I don't want to criticize her!" cried Crane. "I only want to tell her how highly I think of her."

"In my opinion, Burton," Tucker began, when an incident occurred that entirely changed the situation.

A very large elderly gray cat walked into the room, with the step of one who has always been welcome, and approaching Tucker's chair as if it were a familiar place, he jumped suddenly upon his knee and began to purr in his face.

Tucker, under the most favorable circumstances, was not at his best in the early morning. Later in the day he might have borne such an occurrence with more calm, but before ten o'clock he was like a man without armor against such attacks. He sprang to his feet with an exclamation, and drove the cat ahead of him from the room, returning alone an instant later.

"It is outrageous," he said, when he returned, "that our lives are to be rendered miserable by that filthy beast."

"Sit down, Tuck," said Burton, who was talking about wines with the butler. "My life is not rendered in the least miserable. The champagne, Smithfield, ought to go on the ice—"

Tucker, however, could not distract his mind so quickly from the thought of the outrage to which he had just been subjected.

"I must really ask you, Burton," he said, "before you go on with your orders, to insist that that animal be drowned, or at least sent out of the house—"

"Oh, I beg, sir, that you won't do that," broke in Smithfield. "The cat belongs to the cook, and I really could not say, sir, what she might do, if the cat were put out of the house."

"We seem to hear a vast amount about what this cook likes and doesn't like," said Tucker, dribbling a little more hot milk into his half cup of coffee. "The house, I believe, is not run entirely for her convenience."

It is possible that Crane had already been rendered slightly inimical to his friend's point of view, but he was saved the trouble of answering him, for at this moment the cook herself entered the room, in what no one present doubted for an instant was a towering rage. She was wearing a sky blue gingham dress, her eyes were shining frightfully, and her cheeks were very pink.

At the sight of her, all conversation died away.

The butler approaching her, attempted to draw her aside, murmuring something to which she paid no attention.

"No," she said aloud, pulling her arm away from his restraining hand, "I will not go away and leave it to you. I will not stay in any house where dumb animals are ill-treated, least of all, my own dear cat."

It is, as most of us know to our cost, easier to be pompous than dignified when one feels oneself in the wrong.

"Pooh," said Tucker, "your cat was not ill-treated. She had no business in the dining-room."

"He was kicked," said the cook.

"Come, my girl," returned Tucker, "this is not the way to speak to your employer."

And at this, with one of those complete changes of manner so disconcerting in the weaker sex, the cook turned to Crane, and said, with the most melting gentleness:

"I'm sure it was not you, sir. I am sure you would not do such a thing. You will excuse me if I was disrespectful, but perhaps you know, if you have ever loved an animal, how you feel to see it brutally kicked downstairs."

"Preposterous," said Tucker, carefully indicating that he was addressing Crane alone. "This is all preposterous. Tell the woman to keep her cat where it belongs, and we'll have no more trouble."

"It hasn't troubled me, Tuck," answered Crane cheerfully. "But I am curious to know whether or not you did kick him."

"The question seems to be, do you allow your servants to be insolent or not?"

Crane turned to the cook.

"Mr. Tucker seems unwilling to commit himself on the subject of the kick," he observed. "Have you any reason for supposing your cat was kicked?"

"Yes," said Jane-Ellen. "The noise, the scuffle, the bad language, and the way Willoughby ran into the kitchen with his tail as big as a fox's. He is not a cat to make a fuss about nothing, I can tell you."

"I beg your pardon," said Crane, who was now evidently enjoying himself, "but what did you say the cat's name is?"

"Willoughby."

Burton threw himself back in his chair.

"Willoughby!" he exclaimed, "how perfectly delightful. Now, you must own, Tuck, prejudiced as you are, that that's the best cat name you ever heard in your life."

But Tucker would not or could not respond to this overture, and so Crane looked back at Jane-Ellen, who looked at him and said:

"Oh, do you like that name? I'm so glad, sir." And at this they smiled at each other.

"Don't you think you had better go back to the kitchen, Jane-Ellen?" said the butler sternly.

In the meantime, Tucker had lighted a cigar and had slightly recovered his equanimity.

"As a matter of fact," he now said, in a deep, growling voice, "I did not kick the creature at all—though, if I had, I should have considered myself fully justified. I merely assisted its progress down the kitchen stairs with a sort of push with my foot."

"It was a kick to Willoughby," said the cook, in spite of a quick effort on Smithfield's part to keep her quiet.

"O Tuck!" cried Crane, "it takes a lawyer, doesn't it, to distinguish between a kick and an assisting push with the foot. Well, Jane-Ellen," he went on, turning to her, "I think it's not too much to ask that Willoughby be kept in the kitchen hereafter."

"I'm sure he has no wish to go where he's not wanted," she replied proudly, and at this instant Willoughby entered exactly as before. All four watched him in a sort of hypnotic inactivity. As before, he walked with a slow, firm step to the chair in which Tucker sat, and, as before, jumped upon his knee. But this time Tucker did not move. He only looked at Willoughby and sneered.

Jane-Ellen, with the gesture of a mother rescuing an innocent babe from massacre, sprang forward and snatched the cat up in her arms. Then she turned on her heel and left the room. As she did so, the face of Willoughby over her shoulder distinctly grinned at the discomfited Tucker.

Not unnaturally, Tucker took what he could from the situation.

"If I were you, Burt," he said, "I should get rid of that young woman. She is not a suitable cook for a bachelor's establishment. She's too pretty and she knows it."

"Well, she wouldn't have sense enough to cook so well, if she didn't know it."

"It seems to me she trades on her looks when she comes up here and makes a scene like this."

"Beg pardon, sir," said Smithfield, with a slightly heightened color, "Jane-Ellen is a very good, respectable girl."

"Certainly, she is," said Crane, rising. "Nothing could be more obvious. Just run down, Smithfield, and ask her to send up a menu for to-night's dinner." Then, as the man left the room, he added to his friend:

"Sorry, Tuck, if I seem lacking in respect for you and your wishes, but I really couldn't dismiss such a good cook because you think her a little bit too good-looking. She is a lovely little creature, isn't she?"

"She doesn't know her place."

Crane walked to the window and stood looking out for a minute, and then he said thoughtfully:

"If ever I have a cat I shall name it Willoughby."

"Have a cat!" cried Tucker. "I thought you detested the animals as much as I do."

"I felt rather attracted toward this one," said Crane.

III

HIS household cares disposed of, Crane went off to the stables. It was a soft hazy autumn morning, and though he walked along whistling his heart was heavy. These changes in background always depressed him. His mother had been dead about two years, and at times like this he particularly missed her. She had always contrived to make domestic difficulties not only unimportant, but amusing. She had been pretty and young, both in years and spirit, and had had the determining influence on her son since his childhood.

His parents had married early and imprudently. The elder Crane, stung by some ill-considered words of his wife's family, had resolved from the first to make a successful career for himself. Shrewd, hard and determined, he had not missed his mark. Burton's earliest recollections of him were fleeting glimpses of a white, tired, silent man seldom, it seemed to him, at home, and, by his gracious absences, giving him, Burton, a sort of prior claim on all the time and all the attention of his mother.

As he grew older and his father's fortune actually materialized, he began to see that it had never given pleasure to his mother, that it had first taken her husband's time and strength away, and had then changed the very stuff out of which the man was made. He had grown to love not only the game, but the rewards of the game. And Burton knew now that very early his mother had begun deliberately to teach him the supreme importance of human relationships, that she had somehow inculcated in him a contempt not, perhaps, for money, but for those who valued money. Under her tuition he had absorbed a point of view not very usual among either rich or poor, namely that money like good health was excellent to have, chiefly because when you had it you did not have to think about it.

Both her lessons were valuable to a young man left at twenty-five with a large fortune. But the second—the high delight in companionship—she had taught him through her own delightful personality, and her death left him desperately lonely. His loneliness made him, as one of his friends had said, extremely open to the dangers of matrimony, while on the other hand he had been rendered highly fastidious by his years of happy intimacy with his mother. Her wit and good temper he might have found in another woman—even possibly her concentrated interest in himself—but her fortunate sense of proportion, her knowledge in every-day life, as to what was trivial and what was essential, he found strangely lacking in all his other friends.

He thought now how amusing she would have been about the manicured maid servants, and how, if he and she had been breakfasting together, they would have amused themselves by inventing fantastic explanations, instead of quarreling and sulking at each other as he and Tucker had done.

Tucker had been his father's lawyer. It had been one of the many contradictions in Mrs. Crane's character that, though she had always insisted that as a matter of loyalty to her husband Tucker should be retained as family adviser, she had never been able to conceal from Burton, even when he was still a boy, that she considered the lawyer an intensely comic character.

She used to contrive to throw a world of significance into her pronunciation of his name, "Solon." Crane could still hear her saying it, as if she were indeed addressing the original lawgiver; and it was largely because this recollection was too vivid that he himself had taken to calling his counselor by his last name.

He sighed as he thought of all this; but he was a young man, the day was fine and his horses an absorbing interest, and so he spent a very happy morning, passing his hand along doubtful fetlocks and withers, and consulting with his head man on all the infinity of detail which constitutes the chief joy of so many sports.

At lunch, he appeared to be interested in nothing but the selection of the best mount for Miss Falkener—a state of mind which Tucker considered a great deal more suitable than his former frivolous interest in cats. And soon after lunch was over he went off for a ride, so as to get it in before he had to go and meet his new guests.

A back piazza ran past the dining-room windows. It was shady and contained a long wicker-chair. The November afternoon was warm, and here Tucker decided to rest, possibly to sleep, in order to recuperate from a disturbing night and morning.

He contrived to make himself very comfortable with a sofa pillow and extra overcoat. He slept indeed so long that when he woke the light was beginning to fade. He lay quiet a few moments, thinking that Mrs. Falkener would soon arrive and revolving the best and most encouraging terms in which he could describe the situation to her, when he became aware of voices. His piazza was immediately above the kitchen door, and it was clear that some one had just entered the kitchen from outdoors. And he heard a voice, unmistakably Jane-Ellen's, say:

"Stranger, see how glad Willoughby is to see you again. Just think, he hasn't laid eyes on you for all of three days."

Tucker could not catch the answer which was made in a deep masculine voice, but it was easy to guess its import from the reply of Jane-Ellen.

"Oh, I'm glad to see you, too."

Another murmur.

"How do you expect me to show it?"

A murmur.

"Don't be absurd, Ranny." And she added quite audibly: "If you really want proof, I'll give it to you. I was just thinking I needed some one to help me freeze the ice-cream. Give it a turn or two, will you, like a dear?"

It was obvious that the visitor was of a docile nature, for presently the faint regular squeak of an ice-cream freezer was heard. His heart was not wholly in his work, however, for soon he began to complain. Tucker gathered that the freezer was set outside the kitchen door, and that the visitor now had to raise his voice slightly in order to be heard in the kitchen, for both speakers were audible.

"Yes," said the visitor, "that's the way you are. You expect every one to work for you."

"Don't you enjoy working for me, Ranny? You've always said it was the one thing in the world gave you pleasure."

"Humph," returned the other grimly, "I don't know that I am so eager to freeze Crane's ice-cream."

"And Mr. Tucker's, don't forget him."

"Who the deuce is Tucker?"

The listener above sat up and leaned forward eagerly.

"Tucker," said Jane-Ellen, "is our guest at present. He's my favorite and Willoughby's. He has what you might call a virile, dominating personality. Please don't turn so fast, or you'll ruin the dessert."

"How did you ever come in contact with Tucker, I should like to know. Does he come into the kitchen?"

"Not yet."

"How did you see him at all?"

"Owing to his kicking Willoughby down the stairs."

"And you mean to say you stood for that? Why, my dear girl, if any one had told me—"

"Cruel, perhaps, Ranny, but the action of a strong man."

"I think it's a great mistake," said the masculine voice in a tone of profound displeasure, "for a girl situated as you are to have anything to do with her employer and his guests. What do you know about these fellows? How old is this Tucker?"

"Oh, about forty, I should think."

The listener's eyes brightened by ten years.

"What does he look like?"

"Oh, people are so difficult to describe, Ranny."

"You can describe them all right when you try."

"Well," ... Tucker's excitement became intense ... "well, he looks like the husband on the stage with a dash of powder above the ears, who wins the weak young wife back again in the last act."

With a long deep breath, Tucker rose to his feet. He felt like a different man, a strong, dangerous fellow.

"Dear girl," said the masculine voice below him, "you're not going to let this man make love to you."

"Oh, Ranny, he's never tried. He's much too dignified and reserved."

"But if he did try, you would not let him?"

"You, if any one, ought to know that it isn't always easy to prevent."

"I don't know what you mean by that. You've always prevented me, as often as you wanted to."

"Often, but not as often as that. There, Ranny, do get on with the ice-cream. That terrible old woman is coming to stay this evening with her daughter, and you may be sure she'll have us all turned out if everything isn't just right."

"Crane is supposed to be engaged to the daughter," said the male voice.

"Well, I don't envy him his mother-in-law."

"What do you think of Crane?"

There was a pause. At first Tucker feared he might have missed the answer, but presently the question was repeated.

"I asked you what you thought of Crane."

"Oh, I've seen a good many young men of that type in my time," was the reply.

"How strange women are," remarked the ice-cream maker, who had now once again settled down to work. "I should have thought Crane just the man to attract women, well built, good-looking, a splendid horseman—"

"Would you say good-looking?" asked the cook. Tucker had been putting exactly the same question to himself.

But the speaker did not intend to answer it, he went on with his own train of thought: "And here you go into raptures over an old fellow, old enough to be your father—"

"Should you say I went into raptures?"

"You talk as if you were prepared to make an idol of the man."

A pleasant laugh greeted this statement. Tucker grew grave. He did not feel that he thoroughly understood the cause of that laugh, but he took refuge in that comfortable and all-embracing theory that women were fond, unaccountable creatures, particularly when deeply moved.

Another explanation was offered by the man below.

"I believe you are just trying to tease me, Jane-Ellen."

"Trying, Ranny?"

"You know very well you can always do whatever you like with me." The voice deepened with emotion.

"Oh, dear me, no, I can't."

"Why not?"

"I can't keep you turning steadily at that crank. Here, let me show you how it ought to be done."

Tucker knew that she had come out of the kitchen. By leaning over the railing he could see the kitchen door.

He leant over.

The space before the entrance was paved in large square flagstones; here an ice-cream freezer was standing, and over it bent a young man of a somewhat solid build, but with the unmistakable manner and bearing of a gentleman. He straightened himself as Jane-Ellen came out, and watched her closely as she grasped the handle of the freezer; but it seemed to the spectator above that he watched her with other emotions than the sincere wish to learn the correct manner of freezing.

Tucker looked straight down upon her, upon the part in her light brown hair, upon her round little arms, for her sleeves were rolled up above the elbow, as she said didactically:

"It ought to be a steady, even—"

But she got no further, for her pupil without a word, stooped forward and gathering her into his arms, kissed her.

IV

THERE was no doubt whatsoever in the mind of the spectator that this caress, provoked or unprovoked, was not agreeable to its recipient. The young man was large and heavy and she was minute and probably weak, but the violence of her recoil was sufficient to free her within a second.

"'Her strength,'" thought Tucker, "'was as the strength of ten,'" and he hoped it was for the reason alleged by the poet.

She stood an instant looking at her visitor, and then she said, in a tone that no well-trained dog would have attempted to disobey:

"Go away. Go home, and please don't ever come back."

Tucker was deeply moved. It is to be feared that he forgot Mrs. Falkener, forgot his plans for his friend's protection, forgot everything except that he had just heard himself described as a hero of romance by a girl of superlative charms; and that that girl had just been the object of the obviously unwelcome attentions of another. He recognized that the stern but sympathetic husband on the stage would instantly have come to the rescue of the weak young wife in any similar situation, and he determined on the instant to do so; but he found a slight difficulty in making up his mind as to the particular epigram with which he should enter. In fact, he could think of nothing except, "Ah, Jane-Ellen, is the ice-cream ready?" And that obviously wouldn't do.

While, however, he hesitated above, the dialogue below rushed on, unimpeded.

"The truth is," said the young man, with the violence of one who feels himself at least partially in the wrong, "the truth is you are a cold, cruel woman who thinks of nothing but her own amusement; you don't care anything about the sufferings of others, and in my opinion Lily is worth ten of you."

"Then why don't you go and kiss Lily?"

"Because Lily isn't that sort. She wouldn't stand it."

This reply not unnaturally angered the cook.

"And do you mean to say I stand it? I can't help it. I'm so horribly small, but if I could, I'd kill you, Randolph, and as it is, I hate you for doing it, hate you more than you have any idea."

"You know very well it's your own fault. You tempted me."

"How could I know about your silly lack of self-control?"

"You've always pretended to like me."

"Just what I did—pretended. But I'll never have to pretend again, thank heaven. I don't really like you and I never did—not since we were children."

"You'll be sorry for saying that, when you're calmer."

"I may be sorry for saying it, but I'll think it as long as I live."

"I pity the man who marries you, my girl. You've a bitter tongue."

"You'd marry me to-morrow, if you could."

"I would not."

"You would."

"Not if you were the last woman in the world."

"Good night."

"Good-by."

The culprit seized his hat and rushed away through the shadows before Tucker had time to think put the dignified rebuke that he had intended.

There was a pause. He was conscious that an opportunity had slipped from him. He knew now what he ought to have said. He should have asked the young fellow—who was clearly a gentleman, far above Jane-Ellen in social position—whether that was the way he would have treated a girl in his own mother's drawing-room, and whether he considered that less chivalry was due to a working girl than to a woman of leisure.

Though his great opportunity was gone, he decided to do whatever remained. After a short hesitation he descended a flight of steps at one end of the piazza. The kitchen opened before him, large and cavernous. Two lamps hardly served to light it. It was red tiled; round its walls hung large, bright, copper saucepans, and on shelves of oak along its sides were rows of dark blue and white plates and dishes.

Tucker was prepared to find the cook in tears, in which case he had a perfectly definite idea as to what to do; but the disconcerting young woman was moving rapidly about the kitchen, humming to herself. She held a small but steaming saucepan in her hand, which was, as Tucker swiftly reflected, a much better weapon than the handle of an ice-cream freezer.

"Good evening, Jane-Ellen," he said graciously.

"Good evening, sir."

She did not even look in his direction, but bent witch-like over a cauldron.

"I wished to speak to you," he said, "about that little incident of this morning. You must not think that I am by nature cruel or indifferent to animals. On the contrary, I am a life member in the Society for Prevention of Cruelty to them. I love animals." And as if to prove his words, he put out his hand and gently pulled the ears of Willoughby, who was asleep in a chair. Cats' ears are extraordinarily sensitive, and Willoughby woke up and withdrew his head with a jerk.

Willoughby's mistress, on the other hand, made no reply whatsoever; indeed it would have been impossible to be sure she had heard.

"How different she is," thought Tucker, "in the presence of a man she really respects, and recognizes as her superior. All the levity and coquetry disappear from her bearing."

"I was truly sorry," he went on, drawing nearer and nearer to the range, "to have been the occasion—"

"You had better be careful, sir," she said, still without looking at him, "these sauces sometimes boil over." And as she spoke she put a spoon into the pan, and the next instant Tucker felt a small but burning drop fall upon his hand. He started back with an exclamation.

"I am truly sorry, sir," she said, "to have been the occasion—"

He glanced at her sharply. Was she conscious of repeating his own phrase? She seemed to be wholly absorbed in her task. He noticed how prettily the hair grew at the back of her neck, how small and well shaped were her ears. His manner became even more protecting.

"I am an older man than your employer—" he began.

"Yes, indeed, sir."

He decided not to notice the interruption.

"I am older and have seen more of life. I understand more, perhaps, of the difficulties of a young, and I must say, beautiful woman, Jane-Ellen—"

"Why must you say that, sir?" Her eyes fixed themselves on his.

"Because it is the truth, my dear child." He again approached the range, but as a fountain instantly rose from the sauce he retreated and continued: "I would like, if any little troubles in the household arise, to know that you look upon me as a friend, both you and Willoughby." (He thought it not amiss to introduce the comic note now and again.) "I have some influence with Mr. Crane. I should be glad to do you a good turn."

"You can do me one now, sir."

"Pray, tell me what it is."

"You can go away and let me get the dinner."

"You want me to go?"

"The kitchen is no place for gentlemen."

Tucker laughed tolerantly.

"Did you think so ten minutes ago?"

For the second time she looked in his direction, as she asked quickly:

"What do you mean?"

"Your last visitor was not so respectful."

She had put down the saucepan now, and so he approached and tried to take her hand.

Perhaps this is as good a time as any other to describe the sensation of taking Jane-Ellen's hand. The ordinary mortal put out an ordinary hand, and touched something, something presumably flesh and blood, but so light, so soft, so pliant, that it seemed literally to melt into the folds of his palm, so that even after the hand had been withdrawn (and in this instance it was instantly withdrawn) the feeling seemed to remain, and Tucker found himself staring at his own fingers to see if they did not still bear traces of that remarkable contact.

It was just at this moment that Brindlebury entered the kitchen and said, in a tone which no one could have considered respectful, that the motor was coming up the drive.

Tucker was more apt to meet an awkward situation—and the situation was slightly awkward—by an additional dignity of manner rather than by any ill-considered action.

"Ah," he now observed, "in that case I think I must go and meet it."

"I think I would, if I were you," replied the boy, and added to the cook, in case there was any mistake about his meaning: "It seems to me there are too many men in this kitchen in the course of the day."

"Well, goodness knows they're not here to please me," said Jane-Ellen.

Tucker, who understood that this reply had to be made, wished, nevertheless, that she had not made it with such a convincing sincerity of manner. He turned and left the kitchen, and, as he went up the piazza stairs, became aware that the boy was following him.

He stood still at the top, therefore, and asked with that hectoring tone which many people think so desirable to use with servants:

"What's this? You wish to speak to me?"

The boy hardly troubled to approximate civility as he answered:

"Yes; I just wanted to tell you that Jane-Ellen is my sister."

Tucker laughed with indulgent good humor.

"Indeed," he said. "Well, I cannot confess, Brindlebury, to taking a very deep interest in your family relations."

"It's this much interest, that I don't want you going into the kitchen to talk to her."

"Tut, tut," said Tucker. "I think I shall have to report you to your employer."

"And I may have to report you."

This was so beyond the bounds of convention that Tucker thought best to ignore it. He merely turned on his heel and walked into the house, where, in the hall, he found the two Falkener ladies taking off their coats.

Mrs. Falkener was all graciousness. She was engaged in unwinding a veil from her face, and as she freed her nose from its meshes she said briskly:

"And how is the housekeeping going? How is your staff working?"

Crane got them into the drawing-room, where tea was waiting. Mrs. Falkener spoke to him, but she cast a secret glance of question at Tucker. Under most circumstances he would have replied by raising his eyebrows, shrugging his shoulders, closing his eyes, or conveying in some manner the true reply to her demand. But now he merely looked into his teacup, which he was diligently stirring. He found himself uncertain what to do. He had no intention of mentioning the afternoon's incidents to Crane. He did not wish, he told himself, to tell on a poor young woman, and perhaps deprive her of her job. Besides, it is very difficult to tell a story in which you have been an eavesdropper, and tell it with any sort of flourish and satisfaction. The geography of the balcony was such that he would have to confess either to having leaned as far over the rail as possible, or else to having been in the kitchen. But the insolence of the boy Brindlebury put a new face on the matter. He deserved reproof, to say nothing of the fact that he might tell in a mistaken desire to protect his sister from annoyance. To tell any of this to Mrs. Falkener was to put a weapon in her hands which she would not fail to use to get Jane-Ellen out of the house within twenty-four hours. Tucker's first idea was that he did not wish Jane-Ellen to leave the house.

But, as he sat stirring his tea, another thought came to him. Why should she not leave, why should she not become his own cook? Crane, after all, only offered her employment for a few weeks, whereas he—He decided that it would be better for Crane to get rid of her; he decided, as he put it to himself, to be perfectly open with his friend. If Crane turned her out, then he, Tucker, would be there, helpful and ready, like the competent middle-aged hero of the drama, whom she herself had so well described.

He joined but little in the conversation round the tea-table, and Mrs. Falkener, watching him narrowly, feared from his gravity that something serious had happened, that the situation was worse than she had imagined. What, she wondered, had occurred in the last twenty-four hours? What had those evil women with manicured nails accomplished in her absence? She manœuvered two or three times to get a word with Tucker, but he seemed unconscious of her efforts.

When at last they all agreed it was time to dress for dinner, Tucker laid a detaining hand on his host's arm.

"Could I have just a word with you, Burt?" he said.

Crane always felt like a naughty child when his friend spoke to him like this.

"Wouldn't later do?" he asked. "I want to get a bath before dinner, and if we keep it waiting we may spoil some of those wonderful dishes that star-eyed beauty in the kitchen is preparing for us."

"It is about her I want to speak to you."

Both ladies and Crane turned instantly at these words. Then the Falkeners with a strong effort of self-control left the room, and the two men were alone.

"Well, what is it?" said Crane, rather sharply.

Tucker was now all suavity.

"I'm afraid, after all," he began, sitting down and swinging one leg over the other, "that you won't be able to keep that young person.

I'm afraid Mrs. Falkener was right. Women know these things at a glance."

"What things?"

"Why, I mean that in spite of her good dinner, I'm afraid your cook, Burt, is not—Well, I'd better tell you just what is in my mind."

"Surely, if you can," said his host and client.

"I went out for a little while about dusk on the back piazza, which you know is just above the kitchen, and a conversation below is audible there. At first I did not pay much attention to the murmur of voices, but gradually I became aware that some one was making love to Jane-Ellen— "

"Who was it?" asked Crane. "That wretched boy? That smug butler?"

"Alas, no," said Tucker. "If it had been one of the other servants I should not have thought it much harm. Unhappily, it was a young gentleman, a person so much her social superior—Well, my dear fellow, you get the idea."

"No one you knew, of course?"

"I never saw him before."

"How did you see him at all?"

This was the question that Tucker had been anticipating.

"Why, to tell you the truth, Burt," he said, "when I realized what was going on, I thought it my duty for your sake to find out. I looked over the railing—and just at the psychological moment when he kissed her."

Crane was tapping a cigarette thoughtfully on the palm of his hand, and did not at once answer. When he did, he looked up with a smile, and said:

"Lucky dog, is what I say, Tuck."

"I don't think," answered his friend, "that that is quite the right attitude for you to assume."

"What do you think I should do?"

"Dismiss the girl."

Another pause.

"Or," added Tucker, magnanimously, "if you shrink from the interview, I shall be very glad to do it for you."

Crane looked up.

"No, thank you," he said. "I think you have done quite enough. I should not dream of imposing upon you further." He walked to the bell and rang it. Smithfield appeared.

"Tell the cook I want to see her," he said.

After a brief absence Smithfield returned.

"I beg pardon, sir," he said, "but the cook says if she leaves dinner now it will be spoiled, and won't after dinner do?"

Crane nodded.

"You know," said Tucker when they were again alone, "it is not always necessary to tell servants why you are dispensing with their services. You might say—"

Much to his surprise, Crane interrupted him with a laugh.

"My dear Tuck," he said, "you don't really suppose, do you, that I am going to dismiss that peerless woman just because you saw an ill-mannered fellow kiss her? I shall administer a telling rebuke with a slight sketch of my notions on female deportment. It would take more than that to induce me to send her away. Indeed, I was thinking of taking her North with me."

This was a serious suggestion, but Tucker could think of no better way to meet it than to raise his eyebrows; and Crane went off whistling to dress for dinner.

He whistled not only going upstairs, but he whistled in his bath and while he was shaving. The sound annoyed Tucker in the next room.

"It almost seems," he thought, "as if he were glad to see the woman again on any terms." And yet, he, Tucker, knew that she considered Crane quite a commonplace young man—not at all like a hero in the third act.

The way Crane had taken his suggestions was distressing. Tucker did not feel that he thoroughly understood what was in the younger man's mind. His first intention to tell Mrs. Falkener nothing began to fade. It would have been all very well if Burton had been sensible and had been willing to send the cook away and he, Tucker, had been able to engage her, to ignore the whole matter to Mrs. Falkener. Indeed, it would have been hard to explain it. But, of course, if Burton was going to be obstinate about it, Mrs. Falkener's aid might be absolutely necessary.

"After all," he thought, "candor is the best policy among friends."

He dressed quickly and was not mistaken in his belief that Mrs. Falkener would have done the same. She was waiting for him in the drawing-room. They had a clear fifteen minutes before dinner.

"Now tell me, my dear Solon," she said, "just what you think of the situation."

"I think badly of it."

"Yes," said Mrs. Falkener, not yet quite appreciating the seriousness of his tone. "I do, myself. That idiotic housemaid, Lily—I could have told him that name would never do—hooked me twice wrong, and left my daughter's dirty boots on top of her best tea-gown."

"Ah, if incompetence were all we had to complain of!"

"The cook?"

"Is perfection, as far as cooking goes. But in other respect—Really, my dear Mrs. Falkener, I am in doubt whether you should let your daughter stay in this house—at least, until Burton comes to his senses."

"You must tell me just what you mean."

Tucker decided to tell the story reluctantly.

"Why, it happened this afternoon, Burton was away with his horses, and quite by accident I came upon his pretty cook in the arms of a strange young man, a person vastly her social superior, one of the young landholders of the neighborhood, I should say. Seemed to assume the most confident right to be in Burton's kitchen—a man he may know in the hunting field, may have to dinner to-morrow. I don't know who he is, but certainly a gentleman."

"How very unpleasant," said Mrs. Falkener. "Did the woman take in that you had detected her?"

"Yes, and seemed quite unabashed."

"And now I suppose you are hesitating whether or not to tell Burton?"

Tucker was naturally cautious.

"And what would you advise?"

"It is your duty to tell him at once, and get such a person out of the house."

"You think if I told him, he would dismiss her?"

"I am confident he would, unless—"

"Unless?"

"Unless he has himself some interest in her."

"Ah," said Tucker, with a deep sigh, "that's the question."

At this moment Miss Falkener, looking very handsome in a sapphire-colored dress, came in. She, too, perhaps, had expected that somebody would be dressed a little ahead of time for the sake of a few minutes' private talk. If so, she was disappointed.

"Ah, Cora," said her mother brightly, "let us hear how the piano sounds. Give us some of that delightful Chopin you were playing last evening."

Cora, to show her independence of spirit, sat down and began to play ragtime, but neither of her auditors noticed the difference.

"You mean," whispered Mrs. Falkener, "that you have reason to suppose that Crane himself—?"

"Why, to be candid, my dear lady," replied Tucker, "I did tell him. You may have noticed I seemed a trifle abstracted at tea time. I was considering what it was best to do. Well, when you left us, I told him. What do you think he said? 'Lucky dog.' That was all. Just 'lucky dog.'"

"Meaning you?"

"No, no, meaning the fellow who had been kissing the cook."

"Dear me," said Mrs. Falkener, "how very light minded."

"It shocked me—to have him take it like that. And he would not hear of dismissing her. He intends merely to reprove her, so he says. But what reproof is possible? And the most alarming feature of the whole situation is that, to my opinion, he is looking forward to the interview."

"The woman must be sent out of the house immediately," said Mrs. Falkener with decision. "I wonder if higher wages would tempt her?"

"I see your idea," answered Tucker. "You think I ought to offer a position. I would do more than that to save Burt."

"A position as cook, you mean?"

"Why, Mrs. Falkener, what else could I mean?"

"Oh, nothing, Solon, I only thought—"

The friends were still explaining away the little misunderstanding when Crane came down, and dinner was announced.

Mrs. Falkener, with of course the heartiest wish to criticize, was forced to admit the food was perfection. The soup so clear and strong, the fried fish so dry and tender, even the cheese soufflé, for which she had waited most hopefully, turned out to be beautifully light and fluffy. Having come to curse she was obliged to bless; and her praise was delightful to Crane.

"Yes, isn't she a wonder?" he kept saying. "Wasn't it great luck to find any one like that in a place such as this? Tuck, here, keeps trying to poison my mind against her, but I wouldn't part with a cook like that even if she were a Messalina."

Mrs. Falkener, who couldn't on the instant remember who Messalina was, attempted to look as if she thought it would be better not to mention such people in the presence of her daughter.

"Tuck's an inhuman old creature, isn't he, Mrs. Falkener?" Crane went on. "I don't believe he ever had a natural impulse in his life, and so he has no sympathy with the impulses of others."

Tucker smiled quietly. It came to him that just so the iron reserve of the middle-aged hero was often misinterpreted during the first two acts by more frivolous members of the cast.

As they rose from table, Miss Falkener said:

"It's such a lovely night. Such a moon. Have you seen it, Mr. Crane?"

"Well, I saw it as we drove over from the station," returned Crane, a trifle absently. He had become thoughtful as dinner ended.

"Do you think," said Cora, "that it would be too cold to take a turn in the garden? I should like to see the old box and the cedars by moonlight."

"Not a bit. Let's go out. I have something to do first, but it won't take me ten minutes. But," he added, "you must not catch cold and get laid up, and miss the run to-morrow. I'm going to put you on a new Irish mare I've just bought." And they found themselves talking not about the garden, but the stable.

In the midst of it Smithfield came into the drawing-room with the coffee, and Crane said to him, in a low tone:

"Oh, Smithfield, tell the cook I'll see her now, in the little office across the hall."

Smithfield looked graver than usual.

"Beg pardon, sir," he said, "but the cook was feeling tired and has gone up to bed, sir."

Crane was just helping himself to sugar.

"She cooked this coffee, didn't she?" he said.

"Yes, sir."

"She can't have been gone very long then."

"About five minutes, sir."

"Go up and tell her to come down," said Crane.

He turned again to Miss Falkener and went on about the past performances of the Irish mare, but it was quite clear to all who heard him that his heart was no longer in the topic.

Smithfield's return was greeted by complete silence.

"Well?" said Crane sharply.

"Beg pardon, sir," said Smithfield, "Jane-Ellen says that she is very tired, and that if the morning will do—"

"The morning will not do," answered Crane, with a promptness unusual in him. "Go up and tell her that if she is not in my office within ten minutes, I'll come up myself."

Smithfield bowed and withdrew.

Silence again descended on the room. Mrs. Falkener and Tucker were silent because they both felt that thus their faces expressed more plainly than words could do that this was just about what they had expected. But Cora, who was young enough to understand that anger may be a form of interest, watched him with a strangely wistful expression.

After what seemed to every one an interminable delay, Smithfield entered again. He looked pale and graver than any one had ever seen his habitually grave countenance.

"Jane-Ellen is in your office now, sir," he said.

Crane rose at once and left the room followed by Smithfield.

V

JANE-ELLEN was standing in the office, with her hands folded, and an expression of the utmost calm upon her face. Crane came in quickly and would have shut the door, but for the fact that Smithfield was immediately behind him.

"Beg pardon, sir," he said firmly, sliding into the room, "but I must look to the fire."

Crane frowned.

"The fire's all right," he said shortly.

But Smithfield was not to be put off his duties, and began to poke the logs and sweep the hearth until peremptorily ordered to go.

When the door finally closed behind him, Crane stood silent a moment with his hand on the mantelpiece. The whole tone of the interview, upon which it now occurred to him he had rushed somewhat too hastily, would be decided by whether he spoke standing up or sitting down. His feelings were for the first, his intellect for the latter position.

His intellect won. He sat down in a deep chair and crossed his legs. As he did so, the cook's eyes, which had hitherto been fixed on the carpet, now raised themselves to the level of his neat pumps and black silk socks. He was aware of this, but did not allow himself to be disconcerted.

"I suppose you can guess why I sent for you, Jane-Ellen," he said.

"The dinner was not satisfactory, sir?"

"I doubt if you could cook an unsatisfactory dinner if you tried," he returned. "No, the trouble is over something that happened an hour or so before dinner."

"You did not approve, perhaps, of that gentleman, Mr. Tucker, coming into the kitchen? But, indeed, I could not help that."

"Oh," said Crane, "so Tucker was in the kitchen, was he?"

"Yes, sir, until Brindlebury told him the motor was coming with the ladies."

"No," said Crane, "the difficulty is over a former visitor of yours. I think it my right, even my duty to prevent anything happening in this house of which I disapprove, and I do not approve, Jane-Ellen, of strangers coming into my house and kissing the cook."

He looked at her squarely as he said this, but her eyes remained fixed on his feet as she replied docilely:

"Yes, sir. Perhaps it would be better for you to speak to the young man about it."

"Ah," returned her employer, as one now going over familiar ground, "you mean to imply that it was not your fault?"

She did not directly answer this question. She said:

"I suppose in your class of life a gentleman would not under any circumstances kiss a young lady against her will?"

"Well," answered Crane, with some amusement, "he certainly never ought to do so. And by the way, one of the points about this incident seems to be that the young man in question had the appearance of being a gentleman."

"He certainly considers himself so."

There was a pause, then Crane said, seriously:

"I don't want to interfere in your concerns further than I have to, or to offer you advice—"

"But I should be so glad to have you offer me advice, sir. It is one of the few things a gentleman may offer a girl in my position and she accept with a clear conscience."

For the first time Crane looked at her with suspicion. Her tone and look were demure in the extreme. He decided to go on.

"Well, then," he said, "if I were you I would not have a gentleman, especially such an impulsive one, hanging about, unless you are engaged to him with the consent of your family."

She raised her chin, without lifting her eyes.

"It's not the consent of our families that's lacking," she remarked.

"Oh, he's asked you to marry him?"

"Almost every day, sir, until to-day."

"And to-day he didn't?"

"To-day he said he wouldn't marry me, if I were the last woman in the world."

"And what did you think about that?"

"I thought it wasn't true, sir."

Crane laughed aloud at this direct answer.

"And it sounds to me as if you were right, Jane-Ellen," he said. "But, at the same time, I can't see for the life of me why, if you don't mean to marry him, you let him kiss you."

"If you please, sir, it's not always possible to prevent. You see I'm not very large."

Crane looked at her, and had to admit that the feat would be extremely easy. She hardly came to one's shoulder; almost any man—Hastily putting aside this train of thought, he said in a more judicial tone:

"You know your own affairs best. Is the young man able to support you?"

"Yes, sir, very comfortably."

"And yet you don't consider marrying him?"

"No, sir. I don't love him."

Matters had suddenly become rather serious.

"You would rather work for your living than marry a man you don't love?" Crane asked, almost in spite of himself.

For the first time the cook looked up, straight at him, as she answered:

"I think I would rather die, sir."

This time it was Crane's eyes that dropped. Fortunately, he reflected, she could not have any idea how sharply her remark had touched his own inner state. How clearly she saw that it was wrong to do just what he was contemplating doing—to marry for prudence, rather than for love. He found himself speculating on the genesis of the moral sense, how it developed in difficulties rather than in ease. That was why he could learn something on the subject from his cook. Here was a girl working for her living, working hard and long, for wages which though he had once, he remembered, told Reed they seemed excessive, now appeared to him the merest pittance; certainly it seemed as if all the hardships of such a life would be smoothed away by this suggested marriage, and yet she could assert clearly that she would rather die than make it; whereas he, with nothing very much at stake, had actually been contemplating for several months the making of just such a marriage—He was interrupted by her respectful tones:

"Will that be all, sir?"

"Yes," he answered in a voice that lacked finality. "I suppose that's all, except if that fellow comes bothering you any more, let me know, and I'll tell him what I think of him."

Jane-Ellen lifted the corner of her mouth in a terrible smile.

"Oh," she said, "I don't think he'll come bothering any more."

"You're very optimistic, Jane-Ellen."

"I beg your pardon, sir, those long words—"

"Very hopeful, I meant. He'll be back to-morrow."

"Not after what I said to him."

"Well, Jane-Ellen, if you have really found the potent thing to say under such circumstances, you're a true benefactor to your sex."

She looked at him with mild confusion.

"I'm afraid I don't rightly understand, sir."

He smiled.

"It was my way of asking you what you had said to him that you imagined would keep him from coming back."

"I told him I had only pretended to like him, all these years. People, particularly gentlemen, don't like to think you have to pretend to like them."

Crane laughed aloud, wondering if the girl had any idea how amusing she was. In the pause that followed, the sound of a deep masculine voice could be heard suddenly under their feet. The office was immediately above the servants' sitting-room, and it was but too evident that a visitor had just entered.

Crane looked at the cook questioningly, and she had the grace to color.

"Why, did you ever, sir," she said. "There he is, this very moment!"

"Shall I go down and forbid him the house?" asked Burton, and though he spoke in fun, he would have been delighted to act in earnest.

"Oh, no, sir, thank you," she answered. "I am not going back to the kitchen."

This reminded her employer of the extreme difficulty he had experienced in seeing his cook at all.

"Why did you try and get out of seeing me, Jane-Ellen?" he said. "You knew about what I had to say, I suppose?"

"I had a notion, sir."

"And were you afraid?"

At this question, the cook bent her head until a shadow fell upon it, but Crane had a clear impression that she was laughing, so clear that he said:

"And may I ask why it is a comic idea that a servant should be afraid of her employer?"

The cook now raised a mask-like face and said most respectfully:

"No, sir, I was not exactly afraid," and, having said this, without the slightest warning she burst into an unmistakable giggle.

Nobody probably enjoys finding that the idea of his inspiring terror is merely ludicrous. Crane regarded his cook with a sternness that was not entirely false. She, still struggling to regain complete gravity at the corners of her mouth, said civilly:

"Oh, I do hope you'll excuse my laughing, sir. The fact is that it was not I who tried to avoid seeing you. It was Smithfield's idea."

"Smithfield!" cried Crane.

"Yes, sir. He had the notion, I think, that you might be very severe with me, sir, and Smithfield is peculiar, he has a very sensitive nature—"

"Well, upon my word," cried Crane, springing to his feet, "that is exactly what Smithfield says about you. It seems to me I have a damned queer houseful of servants."

The cook edged to the door.

"Perhaps it seems so, sir," she said. "Will that be all for to-night?"

"Yes. No," he added hastily, "I have one more thing to say to you, Jane-Ellen, and it's this. Don't make the mistake of fancying that I have taken this whole incident lightly. I don't. It really must not happen again. Understand that clearly."

"You mean if that gentleman came back, you would dismiss me, sir?"

"I think I would," he answered.

"Even if it weren't my fault?"

"Was the fault entirely his, Jane-Ellen?"

"Ask him, sir."

"You know much more about it than he does. Was the fault entirely his?"

The cook wriggled her shoulders, crumpled her apron and seemed unwilling to answer a direct question directly. At last an idea occurred to her. She looked up brightly.

"It was the ice-cream, sir," she said. "I was trying to teach him how to freeze ice-cream slowly. It ought to be done like this." And bending over an imaginary freezer, she imitated with her absurdly small hand the suave, gentle, rotary motion essential to the great American luxury.

As he stood looking down on her, it seemed to Crane

extraordinarily clear how it had all happened, so clear indeed that for a second it almost seemed as if he himself were in the place of the culprit whose conduct he had just been condemning.

He stepped back hastily.

"No, Jane-Ellen," he said, "it was not all his fault. Of that you have convinced me."

She stretched out her hand to the door.

"Will that be all, sir? The cook, you know, has to get up so very early in the morning."

He tried to counteract the feeling of pity and shame that swept over him at the realization that this young and delicate creature had to get up at dawn to work for him and his guests. The effort made his tone rather severe as he said:

"Yes, that's all. Goodnight."

"Good night, sir," she answered, with her unruffled sweetness, and was gone.

He stood still a moment, conscious of an unusual alertness both of mind and emotion. And that very alertness made him aware that at that moment there was a man in his kitchen against whom he felt the keenest personal animosity. Crane would have dearly liked to go down and turn him out, but he resisted the impulse, which somehow savored of Tucker in his mind. And what, by the way, had Tucker been doing in the kitchen? And Smithfield, why had Smithfield tried to interfere with his seeing the cook? He found plenty of food for reflection.

Among other things he had to consider his return to the drawing-room. Looking at his watch he observed that a longer time had elapsed since he left it than he had supposed. There would be comments, there would be attempted jokes from Tucker. Well, that would be easily met by a question as to Tucker's own interest in the culinary art. Mrs. Falkener's methods of attack were not subtle, either. But Cora—he wished Cora would not just look at him as if he had done something cruel.

But, as is so often the way when we prepare ourselves for one situation, quite another one turns up. The three were not sitting, awaiting his return. The drawing-room was empty except for Mrs. Falkener, who was reading when he entered, and instead of betraying a conviction that he had been too long away, she looked up and said chattily:

"Well, did you reduce the young woman to order?"

"That is a good deal to expect from an unaided male, isn't it?" said Burton, very much relieved.

"Ah, it depends on the male, my dear Burton. You, I imagine, could be very terrifying if you wished to be. What did the young woman do? Weep, protest, declare that it had all taken place quite without her consent?"

Burton smiled. He had no intention whatsoever of sharing his recent experiences with Mrs. Falkener.

"Ah," he said, "I see you know your own sex thoroughly. Where are Tuck and your daughter?"

"Solon is taking a turn on the piazza; he hopes it will make him sleep better; and Cora was tired and has gone to bed." Mrs. Falkener sighed. "Cora doesn't seem very well to me."

"I'm sorry to hear that," returned Crane. "I thought she was looking very fit this evening." He spoke more lightly than he felt, however, for something portentous in Mrs. Falkener's tone struck him with alarm.

"Sit down, Burton," said she, sweeping her hand toward a cushioned stool at her side. "I want to say something to you."

Crane found himself obeying, with his hands between his knees, and his toes turned in, like a school boy who has forgotten his lesson; then, becoming aware of this pose, he suddenly changed it—crossed one leg over the other, as he had done in the office a few minutes before.

In the meantime, Mrs. Falkener was saying:

"The truth is, I'm afraid that we must cut our visit short, delightful as it promises to be."

"Oh, Mrs. Falkener, we're not making you comfortable. What is it?"

"No, Burton, no." Mrs. Falkener held up her hand. "You are making us perfectly comfortable—at least, in all essentials. And who minds roughing it now and then for a week or so? It's good for us," she added playfully. "The housemaid is not—but no matter."

"What has the housemaid done?" asked Crane with what semblance of interest he could summon, but as he spoke his heart went out in sympathy to every hotel and boarding-house keeper in the world. "Good heavens," he thought, "suppose my living depended on my pleasing them, what a state I should be in!" Aloud he said: "What has Lily been doing?"

"Nothing, nothing. Lily means well, I'm sure, in spite of her lackadaisical ways. It is quite a privilege, I assure you, to be waited on by such an elegant young lady. She hooked me up wrong twice this evening, and when I not unnaturally objected, she stuck a pin in me. Oh, by accident, I'm sure. No, I have no fault to find with Lily, whatsoever."

"I'm glad to hear that," said Crane, punctuating his sentence to allow himself to indulge in a half-suppressed yawn. "Who is it, then? Not Smithfield? Or the boy?"

"Oh, I should never have anything to do with that boy," said Mrs. Falkener, bridling. "Oh, never in the world. I think he's half-witted. I saw him stick out his tongue at Solon this evening."

Crane laughed, though he knew he ought not to.

"Did Solon see?"

"No. The boy contrived it so that Solon had just looked away."

"Well, then, perhaps he's not half-witted, after all," said Burton. "It occurs to me that perhaps that is the only reply to a good deal that Solon says."

"I'm devoted to Solon," replied Mrs. Falkener, drawing herself up, "and I must say you ought to—"

"I am, I am," said Crane, hastily, "but I am at the same time able to understand why Brindlebury possibly isn't. But come, Mrs. Falkener, if it isn't these servants that are driving you away, what is it?"

"I don't know how to explain it," said Mrs. Falkener. "It's not really clear to me, myself. I'm sure I don't want to be unkind, or to hurt any one's feelings, least of all yours, my dear Burt." And she leaned over and laid her hand on his. Crane gave it a good brisk squeeze and returned it to her lap as if it were too dear for his possessing; and she went on: "I own I am anxious about Cora. She is very deep, very reserved; she tells me nothing, but she is not happy, Burton."

"I'm sorry for that," said Crane, in a very matter-of-fact tone. He got up and went to a table where the cigarettes were. The profound male instinct of self-preservation was now thoroughly awake, and he knew exactly what he was in for. Only, he noted, that if he had had this interview with Mrs. Falkener before he had seen the cook, he might quite easily have been persuaded that, in the absence of any more definite vocation, he had been created to make Cora Falkener's life tolerable to her. As it was, he saw perfectly that altruism was no sound basis for matrimony.

"You don't understand what it is to be a mother, Burt."

Crane admitted with a shake of his head that he didn't.

"But I have an instinct that this is not the best place for Cora."

"Well, if you were a man, Mrs. Falkener," said Crane, "I should say that that instinct was the result of being poorly valeted. It must be a bore for women to have a wretched maid like Lily. Don't you think that if I found some one a little more competent that you and Cora would feel you could put in at least a week or so with us? The hunting is really going to be good, and Cora does enjoy hunting."

Mrs. Falkener refused to lighten the tone of the conversation. She shook her head.

"No," she said, "no. I'm afraid even a good maid would not help. In fact, to speak plainly, my dear Burton—"

But at this moment the door opened and Tucker came in. His hair was somewhat rumpled by the wind, his hands were still in his pockets as he had had them during his constitutional on the front porch, and his eyes, contracted by the sudden light, looked almost white.

"Well," he said, "are you enjoying this musical party downstairs?"

All three listened in silence, and could hear the strains of "Home, Sweet Home" coming from below.

"They have a phonograph and they are singing in parts," said Tucker, as if this somehow made it worse.

"If we got Miss Falkener down, we might do something ourselves," said Crane, but there was nothing frivolous in his manner when he rang and told Smithfield there was too much noise downstairs.

Smithfield begged pardon and had not a notion it could be heard upstairs. Crane said the boy's, Brindlebury's, tenor carried some distance, and, Mrs. Falkener and Tucker having gone, he added that the house could be shut for the night.

Then he went to the table, and his eye fell again upon the miniature in the pearl frame. He took it up. There was no doubt about it, there was an extraordinary likeness to Jane-Ellen. He smiled to himself.

How very charming she would look, he thought, in a mauve ball dress.

Raising his eyes, he found Smithfield looking at him with an expression he did not thoroughly like.

VI

ON the stroke of seven o'clock the next morning, Burton came downstairs with that exactness which even the most careless man can display in regard to his favorite sport. The rigors of the cub-hunting season being over, the meet did not take place until eight.

Cora was not yet ready for breakfast, and Crane went to fill his cigarette case before starting.

The drawing-room was still dark and in disorder. Crane lit a match to find his way to the table where the tobacco was kept. It was the same table on which had lain the miniature of the lady in the mauve ball dress; and as he held up his lighted match, his eyes sought once more that enchanting pearl circle. The flame died down and burned his fingers before his eyes had encountered what they were looking for. He lit a second match, and then a candle, before he could assure himself that the miniature was really gone.

He sprang into the hall and called: "Smithfield!" with a violence that had little respect for late sleepers.

Smithfield came hurrying out of the dining-room.

"Where's the miniature that used to be on this table?"

"The what is it, sir?"

"The miniature, a picture in a pearl frame."

Smithfield looked thoughtful.

"And what was it a picture of, sir?"

"Of a lady."

"In a black lace cap, and she with white hair, sir?"

"No," said Crane, "she was young and lovely, in a ball dress and a wreath. You must remember it. It was here yesterday."

Smithfield shook his head blankly.

"No, sir," he said, "I can't rightly say that I remember it, but I'll inquire for it."

Crane swore with an uncontrollable irritation—irritation at Smithfield for being so stupid, irritation that he himself had been so careless as to leave the picture about among a houseful of unknown servants.

He was not distracted even by the sight of Cora coming downstairs, looking very workmanlike in her habit with her hat well down over her brows, and her boots, over which Brindlebury had evidently expended himself, showing off her slender feet.

They breakfasted alone; but Burton's mind ran on the loss of the miniature, and he did not really recover his temper until he had mounted Cora, found all the straps of her skirt, adjusted her stirrup, loosened the curb for her, and finally swung himself up on his own hunter, a big ugly chestnut.

The meet was near-by and they were going to jog quietly over to it. They took a short cut across the lawn, and at the sight of the turf, at the smell of the fresh clear morning, the horses began to dance as spontaneously as children will at the sound of a street organ. Crane and Cora glanced at each other and laughed at this exhibition of high spirits on the part of their darlings.

No horseman is proof against the pleasure of seeing one of his treasured animals well shown by its rider; and the Irish mare had never looked as well as she now did under Cora's skilful management. He told her so, praising her hands, her appearance, her understanding of the horse's mind; and she, very fittingly, replied with flattery of the mare and of Crane's own remarkable powers of selection.

They were getting on so well that Burton found himself saying earnestly:

"You really must stay on as long as I do, Cora. Don't let your mother take you away, as she wants to."

The girl's surprise actually checked the mare in her stride.

"My mother is thinking of going away?" she cried.

Well, of course, he wanted her to stay, wanted her, even, to want to stay, but somehow he did not want her to be so much terrified at the thought of departure, did not want her black eyes to open upon him with such manifest horror at the bare idea of departure.

He suggested sending the horses along a little, and they cantered side by side on the grass at the roadside. Crane kept casting the glances of a lover, not at Cora, but at the black mare, as she arched her neck to a light touch on the curb, so that the sunlight ran in iridescent colors along her crest.

Presently they saw two horsemen ahead of them, one of them in that weather-stained pink that, to hunting eyes, makes the most beautiful piece of color imaginable against the autumn fields.

"That's Eliot, the Master," cried Crane. "The hounds must be just ahead. He's a nice old fellow; let's join him. I can't make out who the other one is—no one who was out the last time we hunted."

The canter had given Cora a color. She looked straight before her for a moment, and then she said:

"I think I recognize that other man."

"Who is it?"

"Some one I should like you to know, Burt. His name is Lefferts."

The lane was now too narrow for four to ride abreast. Crane drew Eliot to his side. He wanted to ask him about the Crosslett-Billingtons, for since the disappearance of the miniature, he had made up his mind to investigate the references of his staff. But strange to say, Eliot had never heard of the Billingtons, of their collection of tapestry, or their villa at Capri. He wished to talk of the Revellys.

"A great loss they are to the county, Crane, though, of course, we gain you. I wonder where they are. Gone North, I heard, though I thought I saw one of the boys out the morning of the day you came. The Revellys will hunt anything, from a plow-horse to a thoroughbred. Hard up, you know. Glad they consented to rent their house. Didn't suppose they ever would. Too proud, you know. They have things in it of immense value. Portrait of the grandfather, Marshall Revelly. Second in command to Stonewall Jackson at one time. I'd like to have you know them. Paul, the elder brother, is a man of some ability; may make his mark. And the younger daughter, Miss Claudia Revelly—" Do what he would, Eliot's voice changed slightly in pronouncing the name. "—Miss Claudia is one of our great beauties, the recipient of a great deal of attention. Why, sir, last summer, when Daniel W. Williams, the Governor-elect of this State, saw Miss Claudia at—"

But the story, in which, to be candid, Crane did not take a great deal of interest, was interrupted by Cora who pushed her mare forward in order to attract Crane's attention and to introduce him to her companion.

The young man was extraordinarily good-looking. His eyes were a strange greenish-brown color, like the water in the dock of a city ferry; his skin was ivory in hue and as smooth as a woman's, but his hands and a certain decisiveness of gesture were virile in the extreme.

"We ought to have a good run," said Crane, in order to say something.

"If any run can be good," answered the young man.

"You don't like hunting?"

"I hate anything to do with horses," answered Lefferts, plaintively. "You must admit they are particularly unintelligent animals. If they weren't, of course they wouldn't let us bully them and ride them about, when they could do anything they wanted with us. No, I only do it because she," he nodded toward Miss Falkener, "makes me."

Cora, looking very handsome, laughed.

"He's a poet," she said.

"Is that why he has to hunt?" asked Crane, and he wondered if poetry had anything to do with the excellence of the young man's coat and boots.

"Yes, poets have to be athletic nowadays. It's the fashion, and a very good one, too."

"There are other forms of athletics I don't hate nearly as much," Lefferts went on to Crane, "swimming, for instance, and sailing, and even walking isn't so bad. It doesn't need so much preparation, and getting up early in the morning, and all that sort of thing."

"Fortunately, I know what's best for him," said Cora.

"She makes me think she does," said the poet, still plaintively.

Crane wanted to ask Cora where and how she had acquired this rather agreeable responsibility, but he had no opportunity before they were off.

He and Cora started together, less, perhaps, from chivalry on Burton's part than because of his desire to watch the performance of the mare, but in the course of the run they became separated, and he finally jogged home alone.

He dismounted in the stable-yard and stood watching one of the grooms loosening the saddle-girths, while he and the head man discussed the excellent conduct of his own horses as compared with the really pitiable showing of other people's, and debated whether the wretched deterioration in a certain Canadian bay horse ridden that day by the Master of Hounds was owing to naturally poor conformation on the part of the horse, or deplorable lack of judgment on the part of the rider.

In the midst of these absorbing topics, Crane suddenly became aware that Smithfield was waiting for him at the gateway. He stopped short in what he was saying.

"You wanted to speak to me, Smithfield?"

"When you've finished, sir."

Crane had finished, he said, and turned in the direction of the house with the butler at his side.

"There's been a terrible disturbance at the house, sir, since you went out this morning."

"Oh, my powers!" cried Burton. "What has been happening now?"

Smithfield was stepping along, throwing out his feet and resting on the ball of his foot with the walk that Mrs. Falkener had so much admired.

"Well, sir," he said, "the trouble has been between Mr. Tucker and Brindlebury."

Crane groaned.

"I don't defend the boy, sir. I fear he forgot his place."

"Look here, Smithfield," said Crane, "candidly, now, what is the matter with all of you? You know you really are a very queer lot."

Thus appealed to, Smithfield considered.

"Well, sir," he said, "I think the trouble—as much as any one thing is the trouble—is that we're young, and servants oughtn't to be young. They should be strong, healthy, hard working, but not young; for youth means impulses, hopes of improvement, love of enjoyment, all qualities servants must not have." The man spoke entirely without bitterness, and Crane turning to him said suddenly:

"Smithfield, what do you think about class distinctions?"

For the first time, Smithfield smiled.

"I think, sir," he said, "that if they were done away with, I should lose my job."

"Well, by heaven, if I were you, then," cried Crane, with unusual feeling, "I'd get a job that wasn't dependent on a lie, for if I believe anything it is that all these dissimilarities between rich and poor, and men and women, and black and white, are pretty trivial as compared with their similarities. It's my opinion we are all very much alike, Smithfield," and Crane, as he spoke, was astonished at the passion for democracy that stirred within him.

"That, sir," replied Smithfield, "if you forgive my saying it, is the attitude toward democracy of some one who has always been at the top. There must be distinctions, mustn't there, sir, and you would probably say that the ideal distinction was along the line of merit—that every one should have the place in the world that he deserves. But, dear me, sir, that would be very cruel. So many of us would then be face to face with our own inferiority. Now, as things are, I can think that it's only outside conditions that are keeping me down, and that I should make as good or even better a master, begging your pardon, than you, sir. But under a true democracy, if I were still in an inferior position, I should have to admit I belonged there, which I don't admit at all now, not at all."

"But how about my not admitting that I'm a master?" said Crane.

"In one sense, perhaps you are not, sir," answered Smithfield. "For, after all, some training is necessary to be a servant, particularly a butler, but for the exercise of the functions of the higher classes, no training at all seems to be required. Curious, isn't it, sir? Utterly unskilled labor is found only among the very rich and the very poor."

The conversation had brought them to the house, without the case of Brindlebury having been further discussed. Suddenly realizing this, Crane stopped at the foot of the steps.

"Now, what is it that's happened?" he asked.

Smithfield showed some embarrassment.

"I'm afraid, sir," he said, "that some rather hot words passed. In fact—I do so much regret it, sir, but I fear Brindlebury actually raised his hand against Mr. Tucker."

It was a triumph of self-control that not a muscle of Burton's face quivered at this intelligence.

"If that is true," he said, "the boy will have to go, of course."

"I had hoped you might wish to hear both sides, sir."

"No," answered Crane. "I might hear what Brindlebury had to say, or I might understand without hearing, or I might know that I should have done the same in his place, or, even, going a step farther, I might think him right to have done it, but the fact remains that I can't keep a servant who strikes a guest of mine. That's a class distinction, Smithfield, but there it is."

Smithfield bowed.

"If I might suggest, sir, perhaps you do not understand rightly how Mr. Tucker—"

"Nothing like that, Smithfield. Tell the boy to go, go this afternoon. Pay him what's right and get him out." He ran up the steps, but turned half-way and added with a smile: "And you know there really isn't anything you could tell me about Mr. Tucker that I haven't known a great deal longer than any of you have."

He went in. Tucker and Mrs. Falkener were sitting side by side in the drawing-room, with that unmistakable air of people who expect, and have a right to expect, that they should be given an opportunity to tell their troubles. The only revenge that Crane permitted himself, if indeed revenge can be used to describe so mild a punishment, was that he continued to ignore their perfectly obvious grumpiness.

"Well," he said, "you look cozy. Hope you've had as good a day as we have."

Tucker opened his mouth to say "We have not," but Crane was already in full description of the run, undaunted by the fact that neither of his listeners, if they were indeed listeners, could be induced to manifest enough interest in his story to meet his eye.

"I'm glad some one has enjoyed the day," said Tucker, as Crane paused to light a cigarette. He laid an unmistakable emphasis on the words "some one."

Crane patted him on the shoulder.

"Thanks, Tuck," he said; "I believe that's true. I believe you are glad. Yes, we had a good day—three foxes, and your daughter, Mrs. Falkener, went like a bird. She's a wonderful horsewoman—not only looks well herself, but makes the horse look well, too."

At this Mrs. Falkener's manner grew distinctly more cheerful, and she asked:

"And, by the way, where is Cora?"

Tucker, annoyed at the desertion on the part of his ally, pressed his hand over his eyes and sighed audibly, but no one noticed him.

"I took a wrong turn in search of a short cut and lost the rest of them," said Crane. "But she'll be back directly. She's perfectly safe. She was with Eliot, our neighbor, and a fellow named Lefferts, whom she seemed to know."

"Lefferts!" cried Mrs. Falkener. "That man here! O Burton, how could you leave my daughter in such company? O Solon, you remember I told you about that man!"

Tucker nodded shortly. He wasn't going to take any interest in any one's grievances until his own had been disposed of.

"What's the matter with Lefferts?" said Crane. "He's staying with Eliot, and they asked us all over to lunch to-morrow. Shan't we go?"

"No, nowhere that that young man is," cried Mrs. Falkener, who seemed to be a good deal excited by the news. "He's an idler, a waster. Why, Burton," she ended in a magnificent climax, "he's a poet!"

"So Cora told me."

"He affects to be devoted to Cora," her mother went on bitterly, "and follows her about everywhere, without the slightest encouragement on her part, I can assure you, but I have known him to take a most insolent tone about her. The very first time I ever saw him, he was sitting beside me at a party, and I said, as Cora came across the room with that magnificent walk of hers, 'She moves like a full-rigged ship, doesn't she?' He answered: 'Or rather, more like a submarine; you never know where she'll pop up next. Yes, there's a sort of practical mystery about Cora very suitable to modern warfare.' He called her Cora behind her back, but not to her face, be sure. And very soon a poem of his appeared in one of the magazines—'To My Love, Comparing Her to a Submarine.' I thought it most insulting."

"And what did Cora think?" asked Crane.

"She hardly read the thing through. Cora is far too sensible to pay much attention to poetry."

"But poets are different, I suppose," answered Crane. Personally, he was pleased with the submarine simile.

"No, nor poets, either," said Mrs. Falkener tartly, and rising she hurried away to see if by some fortunate chance her errant daughter had returned without letting her know.

Left alone, Crane decided to give his friend his long-desired chance.

"Well, Tuck," he said, "you look in fine form. What have you been doing since I went away?"

"I have not had a very agreeable day," said Tucker, in a voice so low and deep that it was almost a growl.

"No? Not a return of your old dyspepsia, I hope," said Crane.

Tucker shook his head impatiently.

"At breakfast," he said, "I heard from Mrs. Falkener, who had heard from her daughter, that you had observed the loss of the miniature that used to lie on this table. Such things cannot be taken lightly, Burton. The owners might put almost any price on an article of that kind—wretched as it was, as a work of art—and you would be forced to pay. You see, it could not be replaced. I thought it my duty, therefore, to send for each of the servants and question them on the subject."

"You thought it your duty to send for Jane-Ellen, Tuck?"

Again Tucker frowned.

"I said I sent for all of the servants. Smithfield displayed, to my mind, a most suspicious ignorance and indifference to the whole subject. The housemaid was so hysterical and frightened that if I did not know a great deal of such cases, I should suspect her—"

"And was the cook frightened?" said Crane, with a flicker of a smile.

"No," Tucker explained, "she did not appear to be frightened, but then, I may tell you that I do not suspect the cook of complicity in the theft."

"The deuce you don't!" said Crane. He found himself suddenly annoyed without reason, that Tucker should have been interviewing and questioning his servants during his absence; stirring up trouble, he said to himself, and perhaps hurting the feelings of a perfectly good cook. Suppose she had decided to leave as a result of these activities of Solon's! He found he had not been listening to the account his friend was giving of the conversation, until he heard him say:

"It seems Jane-Ellen had never been in this room before; she was very much interested in everything. I saw her looking at that splendid portrait of General Revelly, and she asked—in fact, she made me give her quite a little account of his life—"

"A little lecture on the Civil War, eh?" said Crane.

His tone was not wholly friendly and Tucker did not find it so. He colored.

"Really, Burton," he said, coldly, "in case of crime, or of theft, a man's lawyer is usually supposed to know what it is best to do."

"Possibly, but I see no point in having dragged the cook into it."

"I see even less point in treating her on a different plane from any of the other servants."

"It almost seems, Tuck, as if you enjoyed your constant interviews with her."

"That is just, I regret to say, Burton, what I was thinking about you."

"It seems to me," said Crane, "that this discussion is not leading anywhere, and might as well end."

"One moment," exclaimed the other, "my story is not finished. When it came to be the turn of that boy Brindlebury, in whom I may as well tell you I have no confidence whatever, his manner was so insolent, his refusal to answer my questions so suspicious—Well, to make a long story short, your boot-boy, Burton, attempted to knock me down, and I had, of course, to put him out of the room.

The situation is perfectly simple. I must ask you either to dismiss him, or to order the motor to take me to the train."

There was a short pause, during which Crane very deliberately lit a cigarette. Then he said in a level tone:

"The boy is already dismissed. He is out of the house at this moment, probably. As to the other alternative—the ordering the motor—I will, of course, do that, too, if you insist."

But Tucker did not insist.

"On the contrary," he said, "you have done all I could desire—more, indeed, for you have evidently decided against the boy before you even heard my side of the case."

"One cannot always decide these cases with regard for eternal justice," said Crane.

Before Tucker could inquire just what was meant by this rather disagreeable pronouncement, Smithfield appeared in the doorway to say that Jane-Ellen would be glad if she might speak to Mr. Crane for a moment.

This was what Crane had dreaded; she was going to leave. His anger against Tucker flared up again, but he said, with apparent calmness, that Jane-Ellen might come in. Tucker should see for himself the effect of his meddling. Tucker suggested in a sort of half-hearted way that he would go away, but his host told him, shortly, to remain.

Jane-Ellen entered. There was no doubt but that she was displeased with the presence of a third party. She made a little bob of a curtsy and started for the door.

"I'll come back when you're alone, sir."

"No," said Crane. "Anything you have to say can be said before Mr. Tucker."

"Oh, of course, sir." But her tone lacked conviction. "I wanted to speak about Brindlebury. He is very sorry for what happened, sir. I wish you could see your way—"

"I can't," said Crane.

Jane-Ellen glanced at Tucker under her eye-lashes.

"I know, sir," she went on, "that there could be no excuse for the way he has acted, but if any excuse was possible, it did seem—" She hesitated.

"You wish to say," interrupted Burton who now felt he did not care what he said to any one, "that Mr. Tucker was extremely provoking. I have no doubt, but that has nothing to do with it."

"Really, Burton," observed his guest, "I don't think that that is the way to speak of me, particularly," he added firmly, "to a servant."

"It's sometimes a good idea to speak the truth, even to servants, Solon," returned Crane. "You are provoking, and no one knows it better than I have known it during the past fifteen minutes. But your powers of being provoking have nothing to do with the matter, except theoretically. The boy has got to go. I want him to be out of the house within an hour. That's all there is to the whole question, Jane-Ellen."

"But, oh, sir, if he is sorry—"

"I doubt very much if he is sorry."

"Oh, why, sir?"

"Because I feel sure that in his place I shouldn't be sorry in the least, except for having failed—if he did fail."

"I know it's a great liberty, sir, but I do wish you could give him another chance." Her look was extraordinarily appealing.

"What in the world is Brindlebury to you, Jane-Ellen?"

"Didn't Mr. Tucker tell you, sir? He's my brother."

"No, he didn't tell me. Did you know he was Jane-Ellen's brother, Solon?"

"Brin told him, himself, sir." She was a little overeager.

Tucker frowned.

"Yes, I believe the boy did say something to that effect. I own I was not much interested in the fact, and I can't say I think it has any bearing on the present situation."

Crane was silent for an instant. Then he said:

"No, it hasn't. He's got to go," and then he added, quite clearly, and looking at his cook very directly:

"But I am sorry, Jane-Ellen, not to be able to do anything that you ask me to do."

She looked back at him for an instant, with a sort of imperishable sweetness, and then went sadly out of the room.

Between Crane and his legal adviser no further words were exchanged.

Crane went and took out one of the motors and rushed at a high rate of speed over the country, frightening one or two sedate black mules, the only other travelers on the roads, and soothing his own irritation by the rapidity of the motion.

More and more he regretted not having been able to grant the favor Jane-Ellen had so engagingly asked, more and more he felt inclined to believe that in Brindlebury's place he would have done the same thing, more and more did he feel disposed to fasten upon Tucker all the disagreeableness of the situation.

VII

HE did not get back until almost dinner time. The meal was not an agreeable one, though Jane-Ellen's part of the performance was no less perfectly achieved than usual. It was evident that there had been a scene between the two ladies. Cora's eyes were distinctly red, and though Mrs. Falkener's bore no such evidence, she looked more haggard than was her wont. Tucker was still feeling somewhat imposed upon, Smithfield's manner suggested a dignified rebuke, Crane felt no inclination to lighten the general tone, and altogether the occasion was dreary in the extreme.

As soon as they had had coffee, Cora sat down at the piano, and drawing Burton to her by a request for more light, she whispered:

"Won't you take me out in the garden? I have something I must say to you."

Crane acquiesced. It was a splendid, misty November night. The moonlight was of that sea-green color which, so often represented on the stage, is seldom seen in nature. The moon concealed the bareness of the garden-beds, lent a suggestion of mystery to the thickets of what had once been flowering shrubs, and made the columns of the piazza, which in the daytime showed themselves most plainly to be but ill-painted wood, appear almost like the marble portico of an Ionic temple.

The air was so still that from the stables, almost a quarter of a mile away, they could hear the sound of one of the horses kicking in its stall, and the tune that a groom was rather unskilfully deducing from a concertina.

Crane whistled the air softly as he strolled along by his companion's side, until she stopped and said with great intensity:

"I want to say something to you, Burton. I'm not happy. I'm horribly distressed. I ought not to say what I'm going to say, at least the general idea seems to be that girls shouldn't—but I have a feeling that you're really my friend, a friend to whom I can speak frankly even about things that concern me."

"You make no mistake there, Cora," he returned.

He was what is considered a brave man, with calm nerves and quick judgment; physical danger had a certain stimulating effect upon him; morally, too, he did not lack courage; though good-naturedly inclined to have everything as pleasant as possible, he was not in the least afraid to make himself disagreeable. But now, at the thought of what Miss Falkener was going to say to him, he was frankly and unmistakably terrified. Why, he asked himself? Young and timid girls could go through such scenes and, it was said, actually enjoy them. Why should he be unreasoningly terrified—terrified with the same instinctive desire to run away that some people feel when they see snakes or spiders? Why should he feel as if prison walls were closing about him?

"Two years ago, when you and I first began to see each other," Miss Falkener went on, in a voice that she kept dropping lower and lower in order to conceal its tremors, "I liked you at once, Burton. I liked you very much. But, aside from that—you know, I'm not always very happy with my mother, aside from liking you, I made up my mind in the most cold-blooded, mercenary way, that the best thing I could do was to marry you."

"Well, I call that a thoroughly kind thought," said Crane, smiling at her, as a martyr might make a little joke about the lions.

"It wasn't kind," said Cora. "It was just selfish. I supposed I would be able to make you happy, but really, I thought very little about you in the matter. I was thinking only of myself. But I've been well repaid for it—" She stopped, almost with a sob; and while she was silently struggling for sufficient self-control to continue, Crane became aware that the front door had opened, letting a sudden shaft of yellow light fall upon them through the green moonshine, and that Tucker had come out on the piazza. He was looking about;

he was looking for them. Not a sound did Burton make, but if concentration of thought has any unseen power, he drew Tucker's gaze to them.

"Burton," said Tucker.

There was no answer.

"Burton!" he called again.

Miss Falkener raised her head.

"Some one called you," she said.

Then Crane's figure became less rigid, and he moved a step forward. He was saved for the time, at least.

"Want me, Tuck?" he said.

Solon came down the steps carefully. He had reached an age when the eye does not quickly adjust itself to changes of light.

"Yes," he said, "I do want to see you. I want to ask you one question. Did you or did you not assure me the boy Brindlebury had left the house?"

"I did so assure you," answered Crane, "and I had been so foolish as to hope we had heard the last of him. Smithfield told me before dinner that he left early in the afternoon."

"Smithfield lied to you. The boy is in bed in his own room at this moment."

"How do you know?"

"Go and see for yourself."

Crane was just angry enough at every one to welcome any action. Only a few seconds elapsed before he was in the servants' wing of the house. All the doors were standing open, disclosing black darkness, except one which was closed, and under this a bright streak was visible.

Crane flung himself upon this, thinking it would be locked, but evidently Brindlebury had not thought any such precaution necessary. The door at once yielded, and Crane entered.

Brindlebury, fully dressed, was lying flat on his back on the bed, with his legs crossed in the air; a cigarette was in his mouth (one of Burton's cigarettes), a reading-lamp was at his elbow, and he was engaged in the perusal of a new novel which Crane had received the day before, and had strangely missed ever since. On the floor near-by was a tray, empty indeed, but bearing unmistakable signs of having been well filled only recently.

Crane took the cigarette from Brindlebury's mouth, and the book from his hand.

"Now," he said, "I'll give you five minutes to get your things together and get out." There were no signs that packing had ever been contemplated; all Brindlebury's belongings were undisturbed.

The boy looked at Crane. He would like to have answered, but he could not think of anything to say, so he got up slowly and tried to smooth his hair which was very much rumpled.

"I'm not positive I have such a thing as a bag," he observed at length, but a little search revealed one in the closet. It was marked "B. Revelly."

"A token of respect from your late employer, I suppose," said Crane.

The boy did not answer. He was rather sulkily putting on his clothes. He was not a neat packer. A tooth-brush and some pipe tobacco, a wet sponge and some clean shirts, boots and pajamas were indiscriminately mixed.

The five minutes, unmarked by any conversation, had almost

elapsed when light steps were heard in the hallway, and a voice exclaimed:

"Did you have a good dinner, honey?" and Jane-Ellen came spinning into the room, all the demureness gone from her manner.

At the sight of her employer, she stopped, and her hand went up to her mouth with a gesture expressive of the utmost horror. Brindlebury did not stop packing. He was now filling in the corners with shaving soap and socks.

His sister turned to Crane.

"Oh, sir," she wailed, "we've acted very wrongly."

"Jane-Ellen," replied Crane, "that really doesn't go. It was a good manner, and you worked it well, but it is now, if you will forgive my saying so, old stuff. I cannot look upon you as a foolishly fond sister, trying to protect an erring brother. I think it far more likely that you are the organizer of this efficient little plan to keep him here unobserved, eating my food, reading my books, and smoking, if I am not greatly mistaken, my cigarettes."

"Oh, Brin, do you take Mr. Crane's cigarettes?" said Jane-Ellen.

"Not unless I'm out of my own," said her brother.

"Without clearing his own honesty, he impugns my taste," said Crane.

It was plain that Jane-Ellen was going to make another effort to improve the situation. She was thinking hard. At last she began:

"I don't defend what we've done, sir, but if you would have let me see you alone this afternoon, I was going to ask that Brindlebury might stay just for this one night. Only I couldn't speak before Mr. Tucker, I'm so afraid of him."

"There you go again," said Burton. "You're not telling the truth. You're not in the least afraid of Tucker."

"Well, not as much as I am of you, sir."

"Jane-Ellen," said Crane, "I believe you are a very naughty girl." He was surprised to find that every trace of ill temper had left him.

"I know what you mean, sir," said the cook, and this time her voice had a certain commonplace tone. "And it's true. I haven't always been perfectly honest with you, but a servant can't be candid and open, sir; you know, yourself, it wouldn't do."

"I'd like to see it tried," returned Crane.

"Well, I'm honest now, sir," she went on, "in asking you to let Brin stay. He'll apologize, I'm sure—"

"I will not," said the boy, still packing.

But his sister hardly noticed the interruption.

"He will do what I tell him when he comes to think it over, if you will only relent. Don't you think you are just a little hard on him? He is my brother, and it would make me so happy if you would let him stay."

The desire to make others happy is not a crime, yet Crane felt nothing but shame at the obvious weakening of his own resolution under the peculiarly melting voice of Jane-Ellen. He glanced at the boy, he thought of Tucker, he looked long at Jane-Ellen. Who knows what might have happened if his eyes, which he decided he must wrench away from hers, had not suddenly fallen upon a small object lying undisguised on Brindlebury's dressing-table.

It was the pearl set miniature.

All three saw it almost at the same instant. The hands of all went out toward it, but Crane's reached it first. He took it up.

"Have you any explanation to offer, Brindlebury?" he said.

"I can explain," exclaimed Jane-Ellen.

"I'm sure you can," Crane answered. "The only question is, shall I believe your explanation."

"He took it because it reminded him of me. That's the only reason he wanted it."

Crane looked from the miniature to the cook. He knew that this was also the only reason why he himself wanted it.

"Jane-Ellen," he said, "go downstairs and order the motor to come to the side door at once."

"Mr. Crane, you're not going to have Brin arrested?"

He shook his head.

"I ought to, perhaps, but I am not going to. I'm going to take him in the motor to what I consider a safe distance, and drop him."

"Just like a stray cat," gasped Brindlebury's sister.

"Cats usually come back," said the boy, with a return of his normal spirits.

"Cats have nine lives," replied Crane, significantly.

Something about the tone of this remark put an end to the conversation. Jane-Ellen obediently left the room. Brindlebury struggled frantically to strap his bulging bag, and succeeded only with the assistance of Crane.

When they went downstairs, the motor was already ticking quietly at the side door. No one was visible, except Jane-Ellen, who was wistfully watching it.

Brindlebury got in, and set his bag upright between his knees; Crane got in, and had actually released the brake, when, looking up at the cook still standing there, he found himself saying:

"Do you want to come, too, Jane-Ellen, to see the last of your brother?"

Of course she did; she looked hastily about and then turned toward the stairs, but Crane stopped her.

"No," he said, "don't go up. There's a coat of mine there in the coat closet. Take that."

Immediately she reappeared in a heavy Irish frieze overcoat he had had made that spring in New Bond Street. It was an easy fit for Crane; it enveloped Jane-Ellen completely. The collar which she had contrived to turn up as she put the coat on, stood level with the top of her head; the hem trailed on the ground, and the sleeves hung limp from below the elbows. She looked like a very small kitten wrapped up in a very large baby's blanket. But she did not allow this superfluity, of cloth to hamper her movements; she sprang into the little back seat, and they started.

After about half an hour, Crane stopped the car. They were now in the outskirts of the main town of the district.

"This is where you get out," he said.

Brindlebury obeyed.

"Smithfield paid you your wages, I believe," and Burton plunged into his own pocket. "Well, there's something extra."

At this, a trembling might have been seen in the right sleeve of the frieze coat, and the next second, Jane-Ellen's hand emerged from the cuff, and Crane for the first time experienced the touch of her fingers. She pushed his hand away from her brother's.

"Don't take that money, Brin," she cried.

Brindlebury's hand dropped.

"No, of course not. What do you take me for?" he said. Then he snatched off his cap and kissed his sister good-by, and, picking up his bag, he disappeared into the darkness.

There was a moment's silence between the other two, before Crane said:

"Better get into the front seat. You'll be more comfortable."

Holding up her coat, as if it were a coronation robe, Jane-Ellen stepped in, sat down, and wrapped it carefully about her knees—a process in which Crane by the greatest effort of self-control did not join. Again the brake squeaked and the motor moved forward.

A great deal has been said about silence as a method of spiritual communion, but few of us, in social situations, at least, have the courage of these convictions. Most hostesses, on looking about a silent dinner-table, would be more apt to think that they were watching a suspension of diplomatic relations, rather than an intercommunication of souls. But there are moments for all of us when we value silence as highly as Maeterlinck himself and this, in Burton's opinion, was one of them.

The moonlight, so much more beautiful and affecting than he had found it earlier in the evening in the garden, the smooth, quick motion, the damp night air blowing against his face, made him acutely aware of the presence at his side of that small, still companion. He felt no need of speech, nor did he speculate as to her state of mind. He drove, and enjoyed life deeply.

They were nearly at home again, before he asked:

"Why was it you did not wish your brother to take what I offered him?"

"Because," she answered, in a tone of simplicity and sincerity he had never yet heard from her, "it would not have been good for him. He's young, and takes things too easily. He ought not to have money he does not work for."

"I am glad that you feel like that," he said. "I was afraid you refused to let him have it, because you were angry at me for sending him away."

He was afraid that she would relapse into her old tone of mock servility and assure him that she would never be guilty of the liberty of criticizing her employer, but she did not. She said:

"But I was not angry at you. I should not have respected you if you had done anything else."

He answered seriously:

"You knew that I was sorry not to do what you asked me to do?"

"Yes, I knew," she said.

They did not speak again.

They left the car at the garage and walked to the house. There had been failure in coöperation, for Smithfield evidently had not known of the expedition. The side door was locked, and so was the front door.

"I suppose I'd better ring," said Crane reluctantly. Somehow he was not eager to face Smithfield's cold, reproving glance.

"No, follow me," whispered Jane-Ellen.

She led him to the kitchen entrance and pointed to a window.

"I don't believe that window has had a bolt for sixty years," she said.

"And to think," returned Crane, as he gently raised it, "that before I took the house I complained of its being out of repair."

He climbed in and opened the kitchen door for her. He had a match, and she knew the whereabouts of a candle. They still spoke in whispers. There was, of course, no real reason why they were so eager to let the household sleep undisturbed, yet they were obviously united in the resolution to make no unnecessary sound.

"Wouldn't you like something to eat?" breathed Jane-Ellen.

"A good idea," he answered.

She divested herself of his coat and beckoned him to the ice-box. They had entirely ceased to be master and servant.

"Some of that chicken salad you had for dinner," she murmured, "if any of it came down. I dare say it didn't though. Smithfield's so fond of it."

Crane laughed.

"You mean he eats in the pantry?"

She nodded.

"All butlers do, and Smithfield's a little bit greedy, though you'd never guess it, would you?"

They laughed softly over Smithfield, as they spread out their simple meal on the kitchen table. Jane-Ellen showed a faint disposition to wait upon her employer, but it was easily vanquished by his assertion that he would eat nothing unless she sat down, too. A few minutes later, it was he who was doing whatever work was to be done, and she sitting with her elbows on the table watching him. There seemed, after all, nothing unnatural in this new relation.

Presently, Willoughby, hearing the sound of dishes, or smelling the chicken salad, awoke and jumped on the table.

"Do you mind him?" asked his mistress in melting tones.

Crane didn't mind him at all. He offered the cat a bit of chicken. Willoughby seemed to enjoy it, chewing it with quick little jerks of his head. And presently, he raised a paw and deflected a fork which Crane was carrying to his own mouth. Even this Crane appeared to find amusing.

Before they had finished, the kitchen clock behind them suddenly and discordantly struck once. Burton started and half turned his head, but she stopped him.

"Let's guess what time it is," she said. "Of course, it's later than half past ten. It might be half past eleven."

"Or even half past twelve."

"It could be one."

"But certainly not half past."

They looked around. It was half past.

Jane-Ellen sprang up.

"Oh, how dreadful!" she exclaimed, without, however, any very real conviction. "How terribly late, and I have to get up so early in the morning."

"It makes me desperately ashamed," said Crane, "to think you have to get up to cook for all of us and that I can sleep just as late as I want to."

She laughed.

"If you haven't anything worse to worry about than that, you're very lucky."

But he had something to worry about, and as soon as she was gone, he began to worry about it, namely, the painful and complicated situation of a man who has fallen in love with his cook.

VIII

MRS. FALKENER never came down to breakfast. At nine to the minute, her bell tinkled, and Lily staggered up to her room bearing a tray, from which, it subsequently appeared, many essentials had been forgotten; the next ten minutes were spent by the unfortunate housemaid in trips to the pantry in search of salt, powdered sugar or a tea-strainer.

Cora, however, came down and poured out coffee for the two men. She looked handsome and vigorous in this occupation, and Crane, sitting opposite to her, wondered if it were his destiny to sit so for the rest of his life. He watched her thin white hands—strong as steel, they were—moving about among the cups. He had once admired them intensely. But now he knew that hands did not have to be so firm and muscular to accomplish wonderful achievements in all sorts of ways.

At ten, Mrs. Falkener came swimming down the stairs, all suavity and brightness. The evening before, while Crane had been struggling with the problem of Brindlebury's misdeeds, she and Tucker had had another council of war. A new attack upon the cook had been planned, which they felt sure would bring to light delinquencies that even Crane could not overlook.

"Come, Burton," she said as she entered the sitting-room, "aren't you ever going to offer to show me the kitchen? You know that to an old-fashioned housekeeper like myself, it is the most interesting part of the whole house."

Such interest, Crane felt inclined to answer, was not confined to old-fashioned housekeepers. Her suggestion roused conflicting desires in him; the desire to see Jane-Ellen, and the desire to protect her from Mrs. Falkener.

"Tuck could tell us all about it," he said slyly.

Tucker, who was reading the paper, pretended not to hear, and presently Crane rang the bell.

"Tell the cook, Smithfield," he said, "that Mrs. Falkener and I are coming down to inspect the kitchen in about ten minutes."

When Smithfield had gone, Mrs. Falkener shook her finger at Crane.

"That was a mistake, my dear Burton," she said, "a great mistake. Take them unaware whenever you can; it is the only way to protect ourselves against the unscrupulous members of their class."

"Crane," said Tucker, without looking up from his paper, "wants to give the young woman plenty of time to smuggle out any superfluous young man who may be visiting her at the moment."

"Well, I'm no gum-shoe man, Tuck," Burton replied, leaving all of his hearers in doubt as to whether or not he had emphasized the word "I."

Tucker laughed sarcastically.

"No, my dear fellow," he answered, "your best friend would not accuse you of having talents along the detective line."

"Perhaps not," replied Crane. "And by the way, did I tell you that the miniature had turned up all right?"

Tucker's face fell. He had depended a good deal on the loss of the miniature as a lever to oust the whole set of servants.

"No," he said. "Where was it discovered?"

"Oh, it had just been moved," answered Crane. "It was lying on another table, when I happened to notice it." He took it out of his pocket and looked at it. "I think now, I'll keep it in my room for safety. You approve of that, don't you, Tuck?"

Tucker, who felt that in some way he was being deceived, would not answer, and in the pause Mrs. Falkener rose and said chattily,

"Well, shall we be off?"

"Coming with us, Solon?"

"No, I'm not," returned Tucker crossly.

"Didn't mean to offend you," Crane answered. "I thought you liked kitchens, too."

Downstairs, they found the kitchen empty. Jane-Ellen was standing just outside the door watching Willoughby, who was exciting himself most unnecessarily over preparations which he was making to catch a bird that was hopping about in the grass near by. The great cat crouched, all still except the end of his tail, which twitched ominously, then he rose, and, balancing himself almost imperceptibly on his four paws, seemed about to spring; then abandoning this method, too, he crept a little nearer to his victim, his stomach almost touching the earth. And then the whole exhibition was ended by the bird, who, having accomplished its foraging expedition, lightly flew away, leaving Willoughby looking as foolish as a cat ever does look.

Jane-Ellen stooped and patted him.

"You silly dear," she said caressingly.

It was Willoughby who first saw Crane. With a vivid recollection of the previous evening's feast of chicken from the salad, the cat ran to him and bumped his nose repeatedly against Crane's legs in token of fealty and gratitude. Burton felt unduly flattered. He lifted Willoughby, who instantly made himself very soft and heavy in his arms and showed every disposition to settle down and go to sleep.

Mrs. Falkener looked at him sentimentally.

"How all animals take to you, Burton, at first sight!" she said.

Crane bent over and replaced Willoughby slowly on the ground, while Jane-Ellen turned her head away for an instant. Mrs. Falkener went on:

"What a nice, bright kitchen you have, Jane-Ellen. A good range, though old-fashioned. How bright you keep your copper. That's right." She wandered away in her tour of inspection. "See, Burton, this blue plate. It looks to me as if it might have value. And this oak dresser—it must be two hundred years old." She was across the room and her back was turned. Crane and the cook stood looking at each other. "How charming, how interesting!" Mrs. Falkener continued. "And you would not believe me when I said that the kitchen was the most interesting part of the house."

"I did not disagree with that," said Crane, still looking at Jane-Ellen.

"Oh, my dear boy, you would never have come down if I had not made you."

"One doesn't always do what one wants to do," said Crane.

Mrs. Falkener turned. The kitchen had revealed none of the enormities she had expected—not even a man hidden in the kitchen closet, the door of which she had hopefully opened; but one chance still remained. The ice-box! In her time she had known many incriminating ice-boxes. She called loudly to be taken to it.

"It's this way, madame," said the cook.

Mrs. Falkener drew Crane aside.

"That," she said, "is the very best way to judge of a cook's economical powers. See how much she saves of the dishes that come from the upstairs table. Now, last night I happened to notice that the chicken salad went downstairs almost untouched."

For the first time in years, Burton found himself coloring.

"Oh, really?" he stammered. "I had an idea that we had eaten quite a lot of it."

"No," returned Mrs. Falkener firmly, "no, a good dish went down. Let us go and see."

Crane glanced at Jane-Ellen. He thought she had overheard.

They reached the ice-box; the cook lifted the lid, and Mrs. Falkener looked in. The first sight that greeted her eyes was the platter that had borne the salad she had liked so much. It was almost empty.

"Why, Jane-Ellen," she said, "where is all the rest of that excellent salad?"

At this question, Jane-Ellen, who was standing beside the chest, gave the lid a slight downward impulsion, so that it suddenly closed with a loud, heavy report, within half an inch of Mrs. Falkener's nose.

That lady turned to Burton.

"Burton," she said, with the majesty of which she was at times capable, "I leave it to you to decide whether or not this impossible young woman did that on purpose," and so saying she swept away up the stairs, like a goddess reascending Olympus.

"Look here, Jane-Ellen," said Crane, "I don't stand for that."

"Oh, sir," replied the culprit, with a return to an earlier manner, "you surely don't think I had anything to do with it?"

"Unhappily, I was watching your hand at the time, and I know that you had."

Jane-Ellen completely changed her method.

"Oh, well," she said, "you did not want her going on any more about the old salad, did you?"

"I don't want the end of my guest's nose taken off."

"It's rather a long nose," said the cook dispassionately.

"Jane-Ellen, I am seriously displeased."

At this the cook had a new idea. She extracted a very small handkerchief from her pocket and unfolded it as she said:

"Yes, indeed, sir, I suppose I did utterly forget my place, but it's rather hard on a poor girl—one day you treat her as if she were an empress, and the next, just as if she were mud under your feet." She pressed the handkerchief to her eyes.

"Jane-Ellen, you know I never treated you like mud under my feet."

"It was only last night in my brother's room," she went on tearfully, "that you scolded me for not being candid, and now at the very first candid thing I do, you turn on me like a lion—"

At this point Crane removed her hands and handkerchief from before her face, and revealed the fact, which he already suspected, that she was smiling all the time.

"Jane-Ellen, what a dreadful fraud you are!" he said quite seriously.

"No, Mr. Crane," answered Jane-Ellen, briskly tucking away her handkerchief, now that its usefulness was over. "No, I'm not exactly a fraud. It's just that that's my way of enjoying myself, and you know, sometimes I think other people enjoy it, too."

"Do you think Mrs. Falkener enjoys it?"

"I wasn't thinking of Mrs. Falkener," replied Jane-Ellen, with a twinkle in her eyes.

"Burton!" called Mrs. Falkener's voice from the head of the stairs.

Crane and his cook drew slightly closer together, as if against a common enemy.

"Do you suppose she can have heard us?" he asked.

"I think she's perfectly capable of trying to hear."

Crane smiled.

"I took a great risk, Jane-Ellen, when I advised you to be candid."

"Burton!" said the voice again.

"Merciful powers!" exclaimed Crane. "She calls like Juliet's nurse."

The cook laughed.

"But you must be prompter than Juliet was."

"What do you know about Shakespeare, Jane-Ellen?"

"Moving pictures have been a great education to the lower classes, you know, sir."

He moved toward the stairs, but turned back to say,

"Good-by, Jane-Ellen."

She answered:

"'Think you that we shall ever meet again?'" and then even she seemed to feel that she had committed an imprudence and she dashed away to the kitchen.

Crane ascended the stairs slowly, for he was trying to recall the lines that follow Juliet's pathetic question, when he suddenly became aware of Mrs. Falkener's feet planted firmly on the top step, and then of that lady's whole majestic presence. He pulled himself together with an effort.

"Do you suppose that girl could have dropped that lid on purpose?" he asked, as if this were the question he had been so deeply pondering.

"I feel not the least doubt of it," returned Mrs. Falkener.

He shook his head.

"It seems almost incredible," he answered, moving swiftly across the hall toward the sitting-room, where Tucker and Miss Falkener were visible.

"On the contrary," replied the elder lady, "it seems to me perfectly in keeping with the whole conduct of this extraordinary young person." They had now entered the room, and she included Tucker and her daughter in an account of the incident.

"You know, Solon, and you, too, Cora, how easy I am on servants. I must admit, every one will confirm it, that my own servants adore me. They adore me, don't they, Cora? No wonder. I see to their comfort. They have their own bath, and a sitting-room far better than anything I had myself as a young woman. But in return I do demand respect, absolute respect. And when I am looking into an ice-box, examining it, at Burton's special request, to have that young minx slam down the lid, almost catching my nose, Solon, I assure you, almost touching my nose, as she did it!"

Tucker listened attentively, tapping his eye-glasses on his left palm. Then he said:

"And what did you do about it, Burton?"

Crane had gone to the bookcases and taken down a volume of Shakespeare. He was so profoundly immersed that Tucker had to repeat his question. This is what he was reading:

> *Juliet:* Think you that we shall ever meet again?
>
> *Romeo:* I doubt it not, and all our woes shall serve
> For pleasant converse in the days to come.

He looked up, vainly trying to suppress a smile.

"What did I do about what, Tuck?"

"About your cook's insulting Mrs. Falkener."

Crane replaced the volume and walked to the window.

"Oh," he said, "I stayed behind a moment—"

"A moment!" said Mrs. Falkener, with something that would have been a snort in one less self-controlled.

At this instant, Crane's attention was attracted by a figure he saw crossing the grounds, and he decided to create a diversion.

"Oh, look!" he exclaimed. "Do come and see the housemaid going out for a walk. Did you ever see anything smarter than she looks?"

The diversion was of a more exciting nature than he had intended. Mrs. Falkener came to the window and uttering a piercing exclamation, she cried:

"The woman has on Cora's best hat!"

"Not really?" said Crane, but it did seem to him he remembered having seen the hat before.

"It is, it is," Mrs. Falkener went on, in some excitement. "Call her back at once. Solon, do something. Call the woman back."

Tucker, thus appealed to, threw open the window, and with an extremely creditable volume of voice, he roared:

"Lily!"

The girl started and turned. He beckoned imperiously. She approached.

"Come in here at once," he said sternly.

Mrs. Falkener sank into a chair.

"This is really too much," she said, making fluttering gestures with her hands. "Even you, Burton, will admit this is too much. Stand by me, Solon."

"Don't say even I, Mrs. Falkener," returned Crane, "as if I had been indifferent to your comfort."

"Don't be so excited, Mother," said Cora. "You know it probably isn't my hat at all. Lily has probably been copying mine."

Mrs. Falkener shook her head.

"I should know a Diane Duruy model anywhere," she said.

At this moment, Lily entered, and good temper did not beam from her countenance.

"I had permission from Smithfield to go out," she began defiantly. "Smithfield sent me over to look up a boy to replace Brin—"

"The trouble is not over your going out," said Crane.

"What is the trouble, then?"

"The trouble," said Mrs. Falkener, seeing Crane hesitate for a word, "is that you have on my daughter's hat."

"Your daughter's hat!" said Lily contemptuously. "Nothing of the kind."

Mrs. Falkener turned to Tucker.

"This is intolerable. This is insufferable," she cried. "To have that woman standing there in Cora's hat, which I chose myself and paid forty-five dollars for at a sale, and cheap, too, for a Diane Duruy model; to stand there and tell me I don't know the hat when I see it—"

"Cora," said Crane, "is that your hat?"

"Why, yes, I'm afraid it is," answered Cora, rather reluctantly.

"Lily, have you any explanation to make?" he asked.

"None at all," replied the housemaid, looking like white granite.

"Cora," said Crane, "you did not by any chance say anything that could have led Lily to believe you meant to give her the hat?"

Miss Falkener smiled.

"No," she said. "My mother would not encourage such a generous impulse in regard to a French hat."

"Then, Lily," said Burton, "take off the hat, and give it back to Miss Falkener, and go and pack your things and be out of the house in an hour."

"You must have her luggage searched," said Tucker.

"Give the hat back!" cried Mrs. Falkener. "What good will that do? Do you suppose that I would ever let Cora put it on her head again, after that woman has worn it? She may as well keep it now."

"I shall," answered Lily. "It's mine."

The girl's determination impressed Crane more than it did the others, though even he could not see any loop-hole of escape for her. He rang the bell, and when Smithfield appeared, he said:

"Smithfield, I have dismissed Lily. We found her leaving the house in one of Miss Falkener's hats."

"Oh, begging your pardon, no, sir," said Smithfield. "It is really not Miss Falkener's hat. Surely, Lily, you explained it?"

"I don't care to speak to them at all," answered Lily.

"Oh, that's no way to speak to your employers, my girl," said Smithfield. "The explanation is this, sir: I understand those great French houses send out many hats alike, sir, and this one was given to Lily by a friend, by Mrs. Crosslett-Billington, to be exact, sir, she thinking it a trifle youthful for herself after she had bought it, and I can't but say she was right, sir, she being a lady now nearing sixty, though hardly looking forty-five. The first evening the ladies came, sir, when Lily had done unpacking their things, she mentioned in the kitchen that Miss Falkener had a hat similar to her own, and we all advised her, sir, under the circumstances, not to wear it during the ladies' stay, as being more suitable and respectful; and she agreed not to, but young women when they have pretty things, dear me, sir, they do like to wear them, and that I presume is why she put on the hat, in spite of our warnings, and I'm sure she regrets it heartily, sir."

"I don't," said Lily. "I'm right glad I did."

"Tut, tut," said Smithfield, "no way to answer, no way to answer."

"Cora," Crane said, "would you go up and see if your hat is in your room?" Cora agreed and left the room at once.

Complete silence reigned until she returned. She was carrying in her hand a hat, the exact duplicate of that which the housemaid wore. They looked from one to another. Lily's triumph was complete.

"Lily," said Crane, "an apology seems to be due to you, which I have great pleasure in offering you, but I must say that if you had been just a trifle more civil, the whole mistake might have been cleared up sooner and more agreeably."

"I think it outrageous," observed Mrs. Falkener, rising. "I think it perfectly outrageous that any servant should own a hat which anywhere but at a special sale must have cost sixty or seventy dollars."

"And now I'll tell you what I think outrageous," said Lily, her soft Southern drawl taking on a certain vigor, "and that is that women like you, calling themselves ladies, should be free to browbeat and insult servants as much as they please—"

"Shut up, Lily," said Smithfield, but she paid no attention.

"No," she said, "no one knows what I've put up with from this insolent old harridan, and now I am going to say what I think."

"Oh, no, Lily," said Crane, taking her by the arm, "you really are not. We're all sorry for the incident, but really, you know you can't be allowed to talk like that."

"But, Mr. Crane," drawled Lily, "you don't appreciate what a dreadful woman she is—no one could who did not have to hook her up every evening."

Between Smithfield and Crane, she was hustled out of the room.

Alone in the hall, Crane and his butler held a consultation.

"She's got to go, Smithfield. Why in the world wouldn't she hold her tongue? Poor girl, I felt every sympathy with her."

"Oh, sir," exclaimed Smithfield, "what shall we do? Jane-Ellen and I really can't run the house entirely alone, sir."

"Of course not, of course not," Burton answered. "You must get some more servants. Get as many as you please—black, white, or red—but for heaven's sake get the kind that won't be impertinent to Mrs. Falkener."

Smithfield shook his head.

"That's a kind will be hard to find, sir, begging your pardon," he observed.

Crane thought it best to ignore this remark.

"I tell you what to do," he said. "Call up Mr. Eliot and say we should all be glad to accept his invitation to lunch to-day if he can still have us. That will give you a little time to look about you. By to-morrow you ought to be able to find some one."

He waited to get Eliot's answer before he returned to the sitting-room, where he saw that Tucker and Mrs. Falkener had had a long, comfortable talk about their grievances and their own general righteousness. He hated to break into the calm that had succeeded by announcing that they were all going out to lunch.

"Burton," said Mrs. Falkener, directing a stern glance at her daughter, "I explained to you yesterday that was an invitation I did not care to accept."

"I know," said Crane, "but my household is now so short-handed that it seemed a question of lunching out or getting no lunch at all.

If you really object to going to Eliot's, I dare say they could give you something cold at home, if you did not mind that. You will come, won't you, Cora?"

"With pleasure," answered Cora.

Crane's manner was unusually decisive, and Mrs. Falkener saw that it was time to make things smooth.

"Oh, no," she said. "No, if you are all going, I shall go, too. Only, home is so delightful, I hate the thought of leaving it."

"It hasn't seemed very delightful to me for the past few minutes," answered Burton, "but I'm glad if you've enjoyed it."

"Ah, Burton, my dear, you take these things too seriously," replied Mrs. Falkener. "A little trouble with the servants—an everyday occurrence in a woman's life. You of the stronger sex must not let it worry you so much. When you've kept house as many years as I have, you'll learn that the great thing is to be firm from the beginning. That's the only criticism I could make of you, Burt, a little weak, a little weak."

Tucker here rose, pressing his hand over his eyes.

"I think, if you don't mind, I won't go," he said. "I've a slight headache. Oh, nothing much, but I'll lunch quietly here, if you'll let me—a slice of cold meat and a glass of sherry is all I shall require."

If Crane were weak, he did not look so at this moment.

"I am sorry, Solon," he answered, "but it would be very much more convenient, if you went with us." He had no intention of leaving Tucker alone in the house with Jane-Ellen, while Smithfield was scouring the countryside for fresh servants.

"I'm not thinking so much of myself," said Tucker, "but of you. I fear I should not be much of an addition to the party."

"But I think of you, Tuck," answered his host.

"What in the world would there be for you to do at home, except talk to the cook?"

Tucker said, rather ungraciously, that of course he would go if Crane wished him to, but that—

Crane, however, did not allow him to finish his sentence.

"Thank you," he said briskly. "That will be delightful. We shall be starting at half-past twelve."

IX

ELIOT'S large library, to which Crane and his party were led on their arrival, looked as only a room can look which has been occupied for several hours by a number of idle men. All the sofa cushions were on the floor, all the newspapers were on the sofas, cigarette ashes were everywhere, and the air was heavy with a combination of wood and tobacco smoke, everybody's hair was ruffled, as if they had all been sitting on the back of their heads, and Eliot, himself, now standing commandingly on the hearth-rug, was saying:

"Yes, and he did not have a sound leg when he bought him, and that must have been in 1909, for I remember it was the last year I went to Melton—" He broke off reluctantly to greet his guests.

Lefferts, who looked peculiarly neat and fresh among his companions, approached Burton, who was beside Mrs. Falkener.

"They have been talking for three hours," he observed, "about a splint on the nigh foreleg of a gray horse that doesn't belong to any of them. Sit down, Mrs. Falkener, and let us have a little rational conversation. Doesn't that idea attract you?"

"Not particularly, since you ask me," replied Mrs. Falkener, not deigning even to look at the poet, but sweeping her head about slowly as if scanning vast horizons.

"The rational doesn't attract you," Lefferts went on cheerfully. "Well, then we must try something else. How about the fantastic-sardonical, or the comic-fantastical, or even better, the—"

But Mrs. Falkener, uttering a slight exclamation of impatience, moved away.

Lefferts turned to Crane, with his unruffled smile.

"She doesn't like me," he said.

"Cora," he added, very slightly raising his voice so as to attract the attention of Miss Falkener, who immediately approached them, "Cora, why is it your mother hates me so much?"

"She certainly does," returned Cora frankly. "You know, Leonard, you are really rather stupid with her. You always begin by saying things she doesn't understand, and of course no one likes that."

Lefferts sighed.

"You see, she stimulates me so tremendously. One gets used to just merely boring or depressing one's friends, but to be actively hated is exciting. People who have lived through blood feuds and tong wars tell you that there is no excitement comparable to it. I feel a little like the leader of a tong whenever I meet Mrs. Falkener. Cora, would you belong to my tong, or would you feel loyalty demanded your remaining in your mother's?"

They went in to luncheon before Cora was obliged to answer, and here Lefferts contrived to sit next to her by the comparatively simple expedient of making the man who had already seated himself at her side get up and yield him the place.

Crane, sitting between his host and another man, enjoyed a period of quiet. Without his exactly arranging it, a definite plan for the afternoon was growing up in his mind—a plan which, it must be confessed, had been first suggested by Tucker's idea of staying at home, a plan based on a vision of Jane-Ellen and Willoughby holding the kitchen in solitary state.

Crane knew that luncheons at Eliot's were long ceremonies. Food was served and eaten slowly, you sat a long time over coffee and cigars, and at the smallest encouragement, Eliot would bring out his grandfather's Madeira. And after that you were unusually lucky if you escaped a visit to the stables, and that meant the whole afternoon.

So he awaited a good opportunity after lunch was over, when Tucker, under pretense of reading a newspaper, had sunk into a comfortable doze, and Mrs. Falkener, while carrying on a fairly connected conversation with Eliot, was really concentrated on preventing Lefferts from taking Cora into another room. This was Crane's chance. He slipped into the hall, found his coat and hat, unearthed his chauffeur and motor, and drove quickly home, sending back the car at once to wait for the others.

He did not, as his impulse was, go in the kitchen way. He did not want to do anything that might annoy Jane-Ellen. At the same time, he rebelled at the notion of having always to offer an excuse for seeing her, as if he were so superior a being that he had to explain how he could stoop to the level of her society. He wanted to say frankly that he had come home because he wanted more than anything in the world to see her again.

The first thing he noticed as he went up the steps of the piazza was Willoughby sleeping in the warm afternoon sun. Then he was aware of the sound of a victrola playing dance music. The hall-door stood wide open; he looked in. Smithfield and Jane-Ellen were dancing.

Though no dancer himself, Crane had never been aware of any prejudice on the subject; indeed, he had sometimes thought that those who protested were more dangerously suggestive than the dances themselves. But now he felt a wave of protest sweep over him; the closeness, the identity of intention, seemed to him an intolerable form of intimacy.

The two were quite unconscious of his presence, and he stood there for several minutes, stood there, indeed, until Jane-Ellen's hair fell down and she had to stop to rearrange it. She looked very pretty as she stood panting and putting it up again, but she exerted no attraction upon Crane. Disgust, he thought, was all he now felt. One did not, after all, as he told himself, enter into competition with one's own butler.

He went quietly away, ordered a horse and went for a long ride. A man not very easily moved emotionally, he had never experienced the sensation of jealousy, and he now supposed himself to have reached as calm a judgment as any in his life. Everything he had ever heard to Jane-Ellen's discredit, every intimation of Tucker's, every sneer of Mrs. Falkener's, came back to him now. He would like to have sent for her and in the most scathing terms told her what he thought of her—an interview which he imagined as very different from his former reproof. But he decided it would be simpler and more dignified never to notice her in any way again. On this decision he at last turned his horse's head homeward.

Smithfield let him in, as calm and imperturbable as ever.

"Your afternoon been satisfactory, Smithfield?" inquired his employer.

Smithfield stared.

"I beg pardon, sir?"

"Have you succeeded in finding a boy to replace Brindlebury?"

The butler's face cleared.

"Oh, yes, I believe I have—not a boy, exactly, quite an elderly man, but one who promises to do, sir."

"Good." Crane turned away, but the man followed him.

"Miss Falkener asked me to tell you when you came in, sir, that she would be glad of a word with you. She's in your office."

Crane stood absolutely still for a second or two, and as he stood, his jaw slowly set, as he took a resolution. Then he opened the door of his office and went in.

Two personalities sometimes advance to a meeting with intentions as opposite as those of two trains on a single track. Crane and Cora were both too much absorbed in their own aims to observe the signals of the other.

"Cora," began Crane, with all the solemnity of which the two syllables were capable.

"Oh, Burton," cried the girl, "why did you leave Mr. Eliot's like that? It has worried me so much. Did anything happen to annoy you? What was it?"

"I sent the car right back for you."

"It wasn't the car I wanted."

Crane began at once to feel guilty, the form of egotism hardest to eradicate from the human heart.

"I'm sorry if I seemed rude, my dear Cora. I thought you were settled and content with Lefferts. I did not suppose any one would notice—"

"Your absence? Oh, Burt!"

He became aware of a suppressed excitement, an imminent outburst of some sort. A sudden terror swept over him, terror of the future, of the deed he was about to do, terror even of this strange and utterly unknown woman whom he was about to make a part of his daily life, as long as days existed. For a second he had an illusion that he had never seen, never spoken to her before, and as he struggled against this queer abnormality, he heard that in set, clear and not ill-chosen terms he was asking her to marry him.

She clasped her hands together.

"Oh, it's just what I was trying to prevent."

"To prevent?"

"Burt, I've treated you so badly."

He looked at her without expression.

"Well, let's get the facts before we decide on that."

The facts, Cora intimated, were terrible. She was already engaged.

"To Lefferts?"

She nodded tragically.

Crane felt a strong inclination to laugh. The world took on a new aspect. Reality returned with a rush, and with it a strong, friendly affection for Cora. He hardly heard her long and passionate self-justification. She knew, she said, that she had given him every encouragement. Well, the truth was she had simply made up her mind to marry him; nothing would have pleased her mother more, but she did not intend to shelter herself behind obedience to her mother; she had intended to do it for her own ends.

"That was what I tried to tell you last evening in the garden, Burt. I deliberately schemed to marry you, but you mustn't think I did not like and admire you, in a way—"

"There's only one way, Cora."

This sent her off again into the depths of self-abasement. She had no excuse to offer, she kept protesting, and offered a dozen; the most potent being her uncertainty of Crane's own feelings for her.

"You behaved so strangely for a man in love, Burt," she wailed, "I was never sure."

"In the sense you mean, I was not in love with you, Cora."

"And yet, you want to marry me?"

"In your own words, I liked and admired you, but I was not in love. The humiliating truth is, my dear girl, that I was so fatuous as to believe that you were fond of me."

There was a short silence, and then Cora exclaimed candidly:

"Aren't people queer! Here I have been worrying myself sick over my treatment of you, and now that I find you are not made unhappy by it, do you know what I feel? Disappointed, disappointed somehow, that you don't love me!"

Crane laughed.

"I also," he said, "have been slightly oppressed by the responsibility of your fancied affection, and I, too, am conscious of a certain flatness in facing the truth."

Cora hardly listened.

"It seems so queer you don't love me," she murmured. "Why don't you love me, Burt?"

At this they both laughed, and went on presently to the more detailed consideration of Cora's affairs. She and Lefferts had met the winter before; she had not liked him at first, prejudiced perhaps by the fact that he was a poet, and that he pretended to dislike all the things she cared for, but she had found, almost at once, that he understood more about the things he hated than most men did about their favorite topics.

"He's really wonderful, Burt," she said. "He understands everything, every one. Do you know, he told me yesterday that I needn't worry about you—that you weren't in love with me. Only I did not believe him. He said: 'What confuses you, my dear, is that Crane is undoubtedly in love, one sees that clearly enough, but not with you.'"

"He did not just hit it there, though," answered Crane, in a rather feeble tone. Cora, however, was in a condition of mind in which it was not difficult to distract her, and she continued without paying any further attention to the example of Lefferts' extraordinary insight. She went on to say that she had had no idea that she was in love, until one day when she found herself speaking of it as if it had always been. Crane asked about Lefferts' worldly prospects, which turned out to be extremely dark. Had he a profession? Yes, such a strange one for a poet—he was an expert statistician, but, Cora sighed, there did not seem to be a very large demand for his abilities.

Among the many minor responsibilities inherited from his father, Crane remembered a statistical publication. He immediately offered its editorship to Lefferts. Cora's answer was to fling her arms about his neck.

"Oh, Burt," she said, "you really are an angel!"

It was Crane's idea of what would have happened if Mrs. Falkener had entered at this moment, which she did not, that made him ask how matters stood in regard to her.

"She doesn't know," answered Cora, "and I don't think she even suspects, and I'm such a coward I can't make up my mind to tell her. Every time I see Leonard he asks me if I have, and now he is threatening to do it himself, and that you know, Burt, would be fatal."

"Cora," said Crane, "I am about to prove that I am no fair weather friend. With your permission, I will tell your mother."

No permission was ever more easily secured.

It was now five o'clock, an hour when the elder lady became restless if not served with a little tea and attention. Crane rang and ordered tea for two served in the office, and then sent Smithfield to ask Mrs. Falkener if he might have a word with her. She and her daughter passed each other on the threshold.

"How cozy this is," she began as she seated herself by the fire. "Smithfield keeps the silver bright, but I'm afraid he has no judgment. Have you seen the man he has engaged instead of that dreadful boy?—why, he's so old and lame he can hardly get up and down stairs. He'll never do, Burton, take my word for that."

"I have something more serious to say to you than the discussion of domestic matters, Mrs. Falkener," said Crane; and for one of the few times in her life, Mrs. Falkener forgot that the house contained such a thing as servants. A more important idea took possession of her attention.

Burton began to speak about romance. He said he did not know exactly how an older generation than his looked at such questions; for his own part, he regarded himself in many ways as a practical and hard-headed man, and yet more and more he found himself gravitating to the belief that romance, love, the drawing together for mutual strength and happiness of two individuals, was the only basis for individual life. People talked of the modern taste for luxury; to his mind there was no luxury like a congenial companion, no hardship like having to go through life without it. Love—did Mrs. Falkener believe in love?

"Do I believe in love, my dear Burt?" she cried. "What else is there to believe in? No girl, no nice girl, ever marries for any other reason. Oh, they try sometimes to be mercenary, but they don't succeed. I could never forgive a woman for considering anything else."

"I thought you would feel like that," said Crane. "I thought Cora was wrong in thinking you would oppose her. For, prudent or not from a worldly point of view, there is no doubt that she and Lefferts are in love."

The blow was a cruel one, and perhaps cruelly administered. Mrs. Falkener, even in the first instant of disaster, saw and took the only way out. Love, yes. But this was not love, this was a mere infatuation on one side, and a dark and wicked plot on the other. She would never forgive Burton, never, for being a party to this scheme to throw her daughter, her dear Cora, into the arms of this adventurer. Burton, who had always professed such friendship for her! She would not stay another moment in his house. There was a six-thirty train to the North, and she and her misguided daughter would take it.

Crane began to see why Cora, for all her physical courage, dreaded a disagreement with her mother. He himself felt as if an avalanche had passed over him, leaving him alive but dazed.

Mrs. Falkener sat with her handkerchief pressed to her eyes, not so much to wipe away her tears, for she was not crying, but to shut out the sight of her perfidious young host.

"Be so kind," she directed from behind this veil, "as to give orders for the packing of my trunks, and let Cora know that we are leaving immediately."

Burton hesitated.

"I am afraid, since the housemaid has left, there isn't any one to pack for you, Mrs. Falkener," he said. "Won't you delay your going until to-morrow? I can't bear to have you leave me like this."

Mrs. Falkener shook her head.

"Call Solon," she said. "No, don't ask me to stay. And why, pray, can't the cook make herself useful, for once?"

Mrs. Falkener was not, of course, in a position to know that Crane would not at the moment stoop to ask any favor of Jane-Ellen. He was glad of an excuse to escape, however, and summon Solon to take his place. He found Smithfield in the hall and explained to him that the ladies were called suddenly away, and then he himself walked down to the garage to arrange for their departure.

When he came back he found the house in the sort of turmoil that only a thoroughly executive woman in a bad temper can create. Smithfield, Cora and Jane-Ellen seemed to be all together engaged in packing. Solon and the new man were running up and down stairs with forgotten books and coats and umbrellas, while Mrs. Falkener was exercising a general and unflattering supervision of every one's activities. To say the new man was running is inaccurate. Even Tucker's dignified celerity hardly deserves such a word. But the new man, crippled and bent as he was, attained only such velocity as was consistent with a perfectly stiff left leg. Crane really felt he ought to interfere on his behalf, when he saw him laboring downstairs with heavy bags and bundles. He probably would have done so, had not his mind been distracted by coming unexpectedly upon a little scene in the upper hall. Cora was trying to press a fee into the hand of Jane-Ellen, and Jane-Ellen was refusing it. Both were flushed and embarrassed.

"I wanted to give you this because—"

"Oh, I couldn't, really; I've not done any—"

"Oh, you've been such a—"

"Oh, no, miss, I've not done—"

The approach of Crane enabled the cook to escape. Cora turned to Burton.

"She's worked so hard, and she wouldn't take a tip," she said. "And you never felt anything like her little hands, Burt. It's like touching a bird."

"Yes, I know," said Crane. "I mean, they look so. I want just a word with you, Cora," he continued, rather rapidly. "I'm afraid I haven't done you much good except that your mother is angrier with me than she is with you, and that's something."

"Oh, I don't care, now it's over," she answered. "And you'll tell Len this evening all that's happened, and where to write to me, and we shall both be grateful to you as long as we live."

At this moment, Mrs. Falkener in hat, veil, and wrap swept out of her room, followed by Smithfield, Tucker and the old man, carrying the last of her possessions. The moment of departure had come.

X

AFTER the departure of the ladies, Tucker and Crane stood an instant in silence on the piazza. Solon, who had been waked from his customary afternoon nap by the frantic summons of Mrs. Falkener, was still a little confused as to all that had happened, and had gathered nothing clearly except that Burton was in some way very much to be blamed.

"It's too bad," he observed, "to have them go off like that. We shall miss them, I fear."

Crane was standing with his hands in his pockets, watching the tail-light as it disappeared down the drive.

"Let us avoid that, Tuck, by going away ourselves."

"You mean to leave here?"

"Why not? The experiment has not struck me as a very happy one. Our servants have gone, our guests have left us, and for my part, I am eager to be off as well."

The time had come, then, when Jane-Ellen was to be friendless and out of a job; the third act was here.

"Anything that suits you pleases me, Burton," said Tucker.

"In that case," answered Crane, "I will telephone Reed to come over at once and make arrangements for giving up the house. We can't, I suppose, catch that night train, but with luck we may get away to-morrow morning."

"You seem in a great hurry."

"I'd like never to see the place again," returned Burton.

In the moment of silence that followed this heartfelt exclamation, a figure came briskly around the corner of the piazza, a figure discernible in the light shed by the front door.

"Oh, come here," said Crane.

The figure betrayed no sign of having heard, unless a slight accentuation in its limp might be so interpreted.

"What's your name?" shouted Burton.

The old man looked up.

"Yes, yes," he said, in a high shaking voice, "I'm lame; you're right there, sir. I've been lame these twenty years, and carrying down all them trunks has put sich a crick in my back as never was."

"I asked you your name," repeated his employer.

"When I came? Why, this afternoon, sir. It was your butler engaged me. I worked at the hotel here once, and Mr. Smithfield he come to my wife and says, 'Susan,' he says, he knowing her since he was a little boy—"

"Let me look at you," said Crane sternly.

But the elderly man, still talking to himself, retreated into the shadow.

And then Tucker was surprised to hear his host exclaim with violence:

"By Jove, the young devil," and to see him hurl himself off the piazza at its highest point. He would have landed actually on top of his decrepit servitor, had not the old man developed an activity utterly unsuspected by Tucker, which enabled him to get away down the avenue with a speed that Crane could not surpass.

"Well, well, what are we coming to?" Tucker murmured as he watched them dodge and double around trees and bushes. Presently they passed out of the light from the house, and only the sound of their feet beating on the hard avenue indicated that the fugitive had taken to the open.

Solon was still peering nervously into the dark when at last his host returned. Crane was breathing hard, and held in his hand a small furry object that Tucker made out gradually to be a neat gray wig.

"Oh," said Burton, still panting and slapping his side, "I haven't run so hard since I was in college. But I should have got him if it hadn't been for his superior knowledge of the ground."

"My dear Burton," said Tucker crossly, "what in the world have you been doing?"

"What have I been doing? I've been trying to catch that wretched boy, Brindlebury, but it's as well I didn't, I dare say. I thought his limp a little spectacular this afternoon when the trunks were being carried down. But his deafness—the young fool!—that deafness, never found anywhere but on the comic stage, was too much for me. He runs fast, I'll say that for him. He led me through a bramble hedge; backed through, himself. That's when I got his wig."

"I should not be surprised if we all were murdered in our beds," said Tucker.

"That's right, Tuck," said Crane, "look on the cheerful side. Come with me now, while I speak to Smithfield. I want to know what he has to say for himself."

Smithfield, looking particularly elegant in his shirt sleeves, a costume which shows off a slim figure to great advantage, was rather languidly setting the dinner-table for two; that is to say, he was rubbing a wine-glass, shaped like a miniature New England elm-tree, to remove the faint imprint of his own fingers.

"Smithfield," said Crane briskly, "I'm afraid your new useful man isn't going to be very useful. He seems to me too old."

Smithfield placed the glass deliberately upon the table.

"He's not so old as he appears, sir," he answered. "Only sixty-six his next birthday."

"A married man?"

"No, sir, a widower of many years. His wife died when her first baby was born—that's Mr. Crosslett-Billington's present chauffeur. That's how I happened to get the old fellow. And when the rheumatism—"

"Smithfield," said Crane, "that's about enough. Put down that glass, put on your coat and hat, and get out. You're lying to me, and you've been lying to me from the beginning. Don't stay to pack your things; you can settle all that with Mr. Reed to-morrow. Get out of my house, and don't let me see you again. And," he added, throwing the gray wig into his hands, "there's a souvenir for you."

Smithfield, without the least change of expression, caught the wig, bowed, and withdrew.

"And now, Tuck," Crane added, turning to his lawyer, "I wish you would go and telephone Reed to come here at once and clear this whole thing up. Tell him I'll send the motor for him as soon as it comes back."

"It's dinner-time now," observed Tucker.

"Ask him to dinner then," said Crane. "I must go and see that Smithfield really gets out of this house."

Both tasks had been accomplished when at about eight o'clock Tucker and Crane again met in the hall. Smithfield had been actually seen off the place, Tucker had telephoned Reed and despatched the motor for him, and now the sound of an approaching car was heard.

"That can't be Reed, yet," said Tucker, "there hasn't been time."

Crane shook his head.

"It isn't the sound of my engine, either," he answered.

Headlights came sweeping up the drive, and a few minutes later, Lefferts, in full evening dress, entered the house.

"I'm afraid I'm a little bit late," he said, "but I missed a turn."

For an instant Crane regarded him blankly. Then he remembered that once, ages before, or perhaps no earlier than that very afternoon, he had invited Lefferts to dinner. And at the same time he realized what had not heretofore occurred to him, that there was no one in the house to serve dinner, except Jane-Ellen, who had, in all probability, cooked dinner for only two. Reed might be there at any minute. It was really necessary, in so acute a domestic crisis, to put pride in his pocket and go downstairs and speak to his cook.

He put his hand on Lefferts' shoulder.

"Awfully sorry, my dear fellow," he said, "that things are not quite as anticipated. Tucker will tell you we have had rather a stormy afternoon. Give him a cigarette and a cocktail, Tuck, and I'll be back in a minute." He disappeared down the kitchen stairs.

With what different feelings, he said to himself, did he now descend those stairs; but, when he was actually in the kitchen, when Willoughby was once again bounding forward to greet him, and Jane-Ellen was allowing herself that slow curved smile of hers, he was surprised and disappointed to find that his feelings were, after all, much the same as before. Over his manner, however, he was still master, and that was cold and formal in the extreme.

"I wanted to speak to you, Jane-Ellen," he began, but she interrupted.

"This time," she said gaily, "I know what it is that you are going to scold about."

"I am not going to scold."

She laughed.

"Well, that's a wonder," and glancing at him she was astonished to find no answering smile. "Are you really angry at me," she asked, "on account of this afternoon?"

"This afternoon?"

"On account of that silly plan about Brindlebury? I did not know they were going to do it, and when it was done, I couldn't betray them, could I?"

Crane made a gesture that seemed to indicate that he really had no means of judging what his cook might or might not do.

"You believe me, don't you?"

"Believe you?" said Crane. "I haven't considered the question one way or the other."

"Why, Mr. Crane," said Jane-Ellen, "whatever has come over you that you should speak like that?"

"This has come over me," answered Crane, "that I came down here in a hurry to give some orders and not to discuss the question of veracity."

The figure of Jane-Ellen stiffened, she clasped her hands behind her back.

"And what are your orders?" she said, in a tone of direful monotony.

Crane, as has been stated, was no coward, and even if he had been, anger would have lent him courage.

"There are two gentlemen coming to dine—four in all," and as he saw Jane-Ellen slightly beck her head at this, he added recklessly, "as Smithfield is gone, you will have to serve dinner as well as cook it."

"No," replied the cook. "No, indeed. Certainly not. I was engaged to cook, and I will cook to the very best of my abilities, but I was not engaged to be a maid of all work."

"You were engaged to do as you're told."

"There you are mistaken."

"Jane-Ellen, you will serve dinner."

"Mr. Crane, I will not."

The problem of the irresistible force and the immovable body seemed about to be demonstrated. They looked each other steadily and hostilely in the eyes.

"We seem," said Crane, "to be dealing with the eternal problem between employer and employee. You're not lazy, the work before you is nothing, but you deliberately choose to stand on your rights, on a purely technical point—"

"I do nothing of the kind."

"What are you doing then?"

"I'm making myself just as disagreeable as I can," answered Jane-Ellen. "Of course, I should have been delighted to do anything for any one who asked me politely. But when a man comes into my kitchen and talks about giving orders, and my doing as I'm told, and serving dinner, why, my answer is, he ought to have thought of his extra guests before he dismissed my brothers—"

"Your brothers!" cried Crane. "Do you mean to say that Smithfield is your brother too?"

"Well, I didn't mean to tell you," said the cook crossly, "but it happens to be true."

From the point of view of the irresistible force, the problem was now completely resolved.

"O Jane-Ellen!" he cried, "why in the world didn't you tell me so before?"

"I can't see what it has to do with things."

"It has everything," he answered. "It makes me see how wrong I have been, how rude. It makes me want to apologize for everything I have said since I came into the kitchen. It makes me ask you most humbly if you won't help me out in the ridiculous situation in which I find myself."

"But I don't see why Smithfield's being—"

"It would take a long time to explain," answered Burton, "although, I assure you, it can and shall be done. Perhaps this evening, after these tiresome men have gone, you will give me a few minutes. In the meantime, just let me say that I was angry at you, however wrongly, when I came down—"

"I'm not sure but that I'm still angry at you," said the cook, but she smiled as she said it.

"You have every right to be, and no reason," he returned. "And you are going to be an angel and serve dinner, aren't you?"

"I said I would if asked politely."

"Though how in the world I shall sit still and let you wait on me, I don't see."

"Oh," said Jane-Ellen, "if you never have anything harder to do than that, you are very different from most of your sex. And now," she added, "I'd better run upstairs and put two more places at the table, for it's dinner-time already."

"If I come back later in the evening, you won't turn me out of the kitchen?"

She was already on her way upstairs, but she turned with a smile.

"It's your kitchen, sir," she said.

Crane followed her slowly. It occurred to him that he must have a talk with Lefferts. He found him and Tucker making rather heavy weather of conversation in the drawing-room. Tucker had naturally enough determined to adopt Mrs. Falkener's views of Lefferts. He had conformed with Crane's request and given the poet a cigarette and a cocktail, but he had attempted no explanation beyond an unsatisfactory statement that the ladies had been called away unexpectedly.

"Nothing serious, I hope," Lefferts had said.

"I hope not," Tucker had returned, and not another word would he utter on the subject.

Lefferts was, therefore, glad to respond to Crane's invitation to come into the office for a few minutes and leave Tucker to the contemplation of his own loyalty.

Left alone, Tucker's eager ears soon detected the sound of dishes in the dining-room, and he knew that this could be produced by the hand of no other than Jane-Ellen. The moment seemed to have been especially designed for his purpose, and he decided to take advantage of it.

Jane-Ellen was setting the table with far more energy than Smithfield had displayed; in fact her task was almost finished when Tucker entered, and, advancing to the mantelpiece, leaned his elbow on the shelf and smiled down upon her benevolently.

"The time has come sooner than we anticipated when I can be of assistance to you, Jane-Ellen," he said.

"Yes, indeed, sir," she returned with a promptness that fifteen years before would have made his heart beat faster.

"Thank you for giving me the opportunity."

"The finger-bowls, sir," she interrupted, flicking a napkin in their direction, "they ought to be filled; not too full, sir; that's quite enough, it isn't a tub, you know. And now, if you've a match about you, and gentlemen always have matches, I believe, would you light the candles, and then, yes, I do think we're about ready now."

Tucker, who could not very well refuse such trivial services when he was offering one much more momentous, poured a little water from the ice pitcher into the glass finger-bowls, but he did it with such dignity and from such a height that he spilled much of it over the doilies. The cook did not reprove him directly, but she changed the doily with a manner that seemed to suggest that another time she would do the job herself. And when Tucker took a neat gold match-box from his pocket and prepared to light the candles, she coolly took the whole thing out of his hands, remarking that he might set the shades on fire and then they'd be in what she described as "a nice way."

Observing that she was about to leave the room, he put himself before the door.

"I want just a word, Jane-Ellen."

"No time now, sir. Perhaps to-morrow morning."

"To-morrow will be too late. You must know this evening. I don't want to say a word against Mr. Crane; young men who have always had everything they want are naturally thoughtless. But I can't bear to see you turned out at a moment's notice—"

"Turned out?"

"Yes, Mr. Crane is going either to-night or to-morrow morning. Didn't he tell you?"

He had her attention now. She looked at him intently.

"Mr. Crane going? I thought he had the house for six weeks."

"So he had, but he's bored with it. Miss Falkener has gone, and he sees no reason for staying on. He'll be off either at midnight or in the morning. You're about to lose your place, Jane-Ellen."

She stood staring before her so blankly that it grieved him to see her so deeply concerned about the loss of her position, and he pressed on.

"I can't bear to think of your comfort being dependent on the caprices of Crane, or any one. Come to me, Jane-Ellen. This is no life for you, with your youth and beauty and charm. I could offer you a position that you need never leave, never, unless you wanted to—"

"Please move from the door, sir."

"Not until you've heard me," and he moved toward her as if to take her in his arms.

At some previous period of time, the Revellys, presided over by a less elegant functionary than Smithfield, must have been in the habit of summoning the family to meals by means of a large Japanese gong that now stood neglected in a corner. To this, Jane-Ellen sprang, and beat it with a vigor that made the house resound.

The next instant Crane burst into the room.

"What's the matter?" he exclaimed, and added, fixing his eyes on his lawyer,

"What the deuce are you doing here, Tuck?"

"I," said Tucker, "was giving Jane-Ellen what help I could in setting the table."

"Like hell you were."

"Do you mean you doubt what I say?"

"You bet I do."

"And may I ask what you do think I was doing?" asked Tucker.

"I think you were making love to the cook."

"Gentlemen, gentlemen," murmured the cook, "won't you please let me go down and attend to the dinner. The chicken will be terribly overdone."

Nobody paid any attention to the request.

"Well," said Tucker, "I certainly wouldn't turn a poor girl out at a few hours' notice, as you mean to do."

"Who says I mean to?"

"You told me yourself you meant to leave to-morrow."

"And what kind of a job were you offering her?"

"I tell you I was trying to help her."

"And is that why she rang the gong?"

"She rang presumably because dinner was ready."

"There's another presumption that seems to me more probable."

"Burton, I shall not spend another night under your roof."

"I had reached the same conclusion."

Tucker turned with great dignity.

"The trouble is," he said, "that you have not the faintest idea of the conduct of a gentleman," and with this he walked slowly from the room.

The cook did not now seem so eager to get back to the kitchen. She stood twisting a napkin in her hands and looking at the floor, not unaware, however, that her employer was looking at her.

"The trouble really is, Jane-Ellen," he said gently, "that you are too intolerably lovely."

"Oh, sir."

"'Oh, sir, oh, sir!' You say that as if every man you knew had not been saying the same thing to you for the last five years."

Jane-Ellen had another of her attacks of dangerous candor.

"Well, a good many have said it, sir," she whispered, "but it never sounded to me as it did when you said it." And after this she had the grace to dart through the door and downstairs, so fast that he could hear her little heels clatter on each step as she went.

In the hall he found Tucker, standing under a lamp, studying a time-table, with glasses set very far down his nose. Opposite, Lefferts was leaning against the wall, his arms folded and the expression on his face of one who has happened unexpectedly upon a very good moving picture show.

Seeing Crane, Tucker folded up his time-table and removed his glasses.

"Your other guest has just arrived," he observed.

"Oh, is Reed here?"

"Yes," said Lefferts, "he's in your office taking off his coat."

"And you may be interested to know," added Tucker, with a biting simplicity that had impressed many juries in its time, "you may be interested to know that he is the man I found kissing Jane-Ellen last week."

"What, Reed!" cried Crane, with a gesture that might have been interpreted as ferocious.

Hearing his name called, Reed came hurrying out.

"Yes," he said, advancing with outstretched hand, "here I am. Sorry to be late, but I was ready before—"

"We'll go in to dinner," said Crane shortly. Tucker and Reed moved first toward the dining-room. Lefferts drew his host aside.

"Just one moment," he said. "You went off so quickly when that gong rang that I did not have any chance to tell you how I feel about your generosity. It makes—"

Crane grasped his hand.

"You have an opportunity this very moment," he replied, "to repay me for anything I ever have done or may do for you. Talk, my dear fellow, talk at dinner. Do nothing but talk. Otherwise, I shall knock those two men's heads together."

Lefferts smiled.

"I doubt if you'd get much sense into them even if you did," he murmured.

"No," answered Burton, "but I should have a great deal of enjoyment in doing it."

XI

THEY sat down at table, and, as Crane looked at his guests, he had little hope that even Lefferts' cheerful facility could save the situation. Circumstances would be too much against him. Even the poet himself could hardly be at his best, having just arrived in the hope of dining with his lady-love to find she had been spirited away by an irate mother. This in itself was enough to put a pall on most men; yet, of the three guests, Lefferts seemed by far the most hopeful. Tucker was already sullen and getting more sullen every moment. Crane knew the signs of his lawyer's bearing—the irritable eye that would meet no one's directly, the tapping fingers, the lips compressed but moving. Tucker was one of those people cursed by anger after the event. His nature, slow moving or overcontrolled, bore him past the real moment of offense without explosion; but with the crisis over, his resentment began to gain in strength and to grow more bitter as the opportunity for action receded more and more into the past. Crane knew now that Tucker was reviewing every phrase that had passed between them; every injury, real or fancied, that he had ever received at Crane's hands; these he was summoning like a sort of phantom army to fight on his side. No, Tucker was not a guest from whom any host could expect much genial interchange that evening.

Reed, on the other hand, was too unconscious. Placid, good-natured, confident in his own powers to arrange any little domestic difficulties that might have arisen, he sat down, unfolded his napkin, and turned to Lefferts in answer to the inquiry about real estate which Lefferts had just tactfully addressed to him.

"The great charm of this section of the country," he was saying, "is that from the time of its earliest settlement it has been in the hands of a small group of—" At this instant Jane-Ellen entered with the soup. Reed, who had expected to see Smithfield, stopped short, and stared at her with an astonishment he did not even attempt to disguise. Lefferts, following the direction of his eyes and seeing Jane-Ellen for the first time, mistook the subject of Reed's surprise.

"Oh," he said, as the girl left the room, "is this 'the face that launched a thousand ships'?"

Tucker, who was perhaps not as familiar with the Elizabethan dramatists as he should have been, replied shortly that this was the cook.

"A very beautiful little person," said Lefferts, imagining, poor fellow, that he was now on safe ground.

"I own," said Tucker, "that I have never been able to take much interest in the personal appearance of servants."

"You sometimes behave as if you did, Tuck," remarked his host.

"If you are interested in beauty," observed Lefferts, "I don't see how you can eliminate any of its manifestations, particularly according to social classes."

"Such a preoccupation with beauty strikes me as decadent," answered Tucker crossly.

"Indeed, how delightful," Lefferts replied. "What, exactly, is your definition of 'decadent'?"

Now in Tucker's vocabulary the word "decadent" was a hate word. It signified nothing definite, except that he disliked the person to whose opinions he applied it. He had several others of the same sort—hysterical, half-baked and subversive-of-the-Constitution being those most often in use. This being so, he really couldn't define the word, and so he pretended not to hear and occupied himself flicking an imaginary crumb from the satin lapel of his coat.

Lefferts, who had no wish to be disagreeable, did not repeat the question, but contented himself by observing that he had never tasted such delicious soup. Reed shook his head in an ecstasy that seemed to transcend words. Only Tucker scowled.

As Jane-Ellen entered at this moment to take away the soup-plates, Crane, who was growing reckless, decided to let her share the compliment.

"The gentlemen enjoyed the soup, Jane-Ellen," he said, "at least, Mr. Lefferts and Mr. Reed did, but Mr. Tucker has not committed himself. Did you enjoy the soup, Tuck?"

Tucker rapped with his middle finger.

"I care very little for my food," he answered.

"Well," said Crane, "I've heard of hating the sin and loving the sinner; I suppose it is possible to hate the cooking and—and—" He paused.

"I did not say I hated the cooking," answered Tucker. "I only say I am not interested in talking about it all the time."

"All right," said Burton, "we'll talk about something else, and you shall have first choice of a topic, Tuck."

"One moment before we begin," exclaimed Reed, "I must ask, where is Smithfield?"

Crane turned to him.

"Smithfield," he said, "in common with my two guests, the housemaid Lily and the boy Brindlebury, have all left, or been ejected from my house within the last twenty-four hours."

"You mean," gasped Reed, "that you and Mr. Tucker and the cook are alone in the house!"

"I regret to say that Mr. Tucker also leaves me this evening."

"But—but—" began Reed, in a protest too earnest to find words on the instant.

"We won't discuss the matter now," said Crane. "I have several things to talk over with you, Mr. Reed, after dinner. In the meantime," he added, looking around on the dreary faces of all but Lefferts, "let us enjoy ourselves."

"Certainly, by all means," agreed Reed, "but I would just like to ask you, Mr. Crane—You can't mean, you don't intend, you don't contemplate—"

"Oh, I won't trouble you with my immediate plans," said Crane, and added, turning to Lefferts, "my experience is that no one is really interested in any one else's plans—their daily routine, I mean, and small domestic complications."

"Oh, come, I don't know about that," answered Lefferts, on whom the situation was beginning vaguely to dawn. "Mr. Reed struck me as being very genuinely interested in your intentions. You are genuinely interested, aren't you, Mr. Reed?"

Reed was interested beyond the point of being able to suspect malice.

"Yes, yes," he said eagerly, "I am, genuinely, sincerely. You see, I understand what would be said in a community like this,—what would be thought. You get my idea?"

"I own I don't," answered Burton suavely, "but I will say this much, that in deciding my conduct, I have usually considered my own opinion rather than that of others."

"Of course, exactly. I do, myself," said Reed, "but in this case, I really think you would agree with me if I could make myself clear."

"Doubtless, doubtless," answered Crane, and seeing that Jane-Ellen was again in the room, he went on: "What is it exactly that we are talking about? What is it that you fear?"

Reed cast an agonized look at the cook and remained speechless, but Tucker, with more experience in the befogging properties of language, rushed to his assistance.

"It's perfectly clear what he means," he said. "Mr. Reed's idea is that in a small community like this the conduct of every individual is watched, scrutinized and discussed, however humble a sphere he or she may occupy; and that if any young woman should find herself in a position which has been considered a compromising one by every author and dramatist in the language, she would not be saved from the inevitable criticism that would follow by the mere fact that—"

But here something very unfortunate happened. The lip of the ice-water pitcher, which Jane-Ellen was approaching to Tucker's glass, suddenly touched his shoulder, and a small quantity of the chilling liquid trickled between his collar and his neck. It was not enough to be called a stream, and yet it was distinctly more than a drop; it was sufficient to cut short his sentence.

"Oh, sir, I'm so sorry," she cried, and she added, with a sort of wail, looking at Crane, "You see how it is, sir, I'm not used to waiting on table."

"I think she waits admirably," murmured Lefferts aside to his host.

"Extremely competent, I call it," said Crane clearly. "Don't give it another thought, Jane-Ellen. See," he added, glancing at Tucker's face which was distorted with anger, "Mr. Tucker has forgotten it already."

"Oh, sir, how kind you are to me!" cried the cook and ran hastily into the pantry, from which a sound which might have been a cough was instantly heard.

"Yours is a strange but delightful home, Crane," observed Lefferts. "I don't really recall ever having experienced anything quite like it."

"You refer, I fancy," replied Crane, "to the simple peace, the assured confidence that—"

"That something unexpected is going to happen within the next ten seconds."

Tucker and Reed, both absorbed in their private wrongs, were for an instant like deaf men, but the latter having now dried his neck and as much of his collar as was possible, showed signs of coming to, so that Crane included both in the conversation.

"Lefferts and I were speaking," he said, slightly raising his voice, "of the peculiar atmosphere that makes for the enjoyment of a home. What, Mr. Reed, do you think is most essential?"

"Just one moment, Mr. Crane," said Reed. "I want to say a word more of that other subject we were speaking of."

Crane's seat allowed him to see the pantry door before any one else could. On it his eyes were fixed as he answered thoughtfully:

"Our last subject. Now, let me see, what was that?"

"It was the question of the propriety of—"

"Fish, sir?" said a gentle voice in Reed's ear. He groaned and helped himself largely and in silence.

Lefferts, who was really kind-hearted, pitied his distress and decided to change the topic.

"What a fine old house this is," he said, glancing around the high-ceilinged room. "Who does it belong to?"

"It belongs," answered Tucker, "to a family named Revelly—a family who held a highly honored position in the history of our country until they took the wrong side in war."

"In this part of the country, sir," cried Reed, "we are not accustomed to thinking it the wrong side."

Tucker bowed slightly.

"I believe that I am voicing the verdict of history and time," he answered.

It was in remorse, perhaps, for having stirred up this new subject of dispute that Lefferts now went on rapidly, too rapidly to feel his way.

"Well, this present generation seems to be an amusing lot. Eliot was telling me about them last night. He says one of the girls is a perfect beauty. Now, what was her name—such a pretty one. Oh, yes," he added, slightly raising his voice, as his memory gave it to him, "Claudia."

"What?" said the cook.

"Nobody spoke to you, Jane-Ellen," said Crane, but his eyes remained fixed on her long and meditatively as she handed the sauce for the fish.

Lefferts continued:

"Eliot said that she was a most indiscriminating fascinator—engaged to three men last summer, to his knowledge. Our Northern girls are infants compared—"

Reed suddenly sprang up from the table.

"I'd be obliged, sir," he said, "if you'd tell Mr. Eliot, with my compliments, that that story of his is untrue, and if he doesn't know it, he ought to. I don't blame you, sir, a stranger, for repeating all you hear about one of the loveliest young ladies in the country, but I do blame him—"

At this the cook approached him and said with a stern civility:

"Do sit down and eat your fish, sir, before it gets cold." They exchanged a long and bitter glance, but Reed sat down.

"I'm sure you'll believe," said Lefferts, "that I'm sorry to have said anything I ought not, particularly about any friend of yours, Mr. Reed, but the truth is, I thought of it only as being immensely to the credit of the young lady, in a neighborhood which must be, you'll forgive my saying, rather dull if you're not fond of hunting."

"The point is not whether it is to her credit or not," returned Reed, who was by no means placated, "the point is that it is not true."

"Probably not," Lefferts agreed, "only," he added, after a second's thought, "I don't see how any one can say that except the young lady herself."

"Miss Claudia Revelly," answered Reed, "is one of the most respected and admired young ladies in the State, I may say in the whole South. I have known her and her family since she was a child, and I should have been informed if anything of the kind had taken place."

As he said this, the glance that the cook cast at him was indescribable. It was mingled pity and wonder, as much as to say, "What hope is there, after all, for a man who can talk like that?"

"Undoubtedly you're right, Mr. Reed," said Lefferts, "and yet I have never heard of a girl's announcing more than one engagement at a time, although it has come within my experience to know—"

"But, after all, why not?" said Crane. "Perhaps that will be the coming fashion. We shall in future get letters from our friends, which will begin: 'I want you to know of the three great happinesses that have come into my life. I am engaged to John Jones, Peter Smith and Paul Robinson, and I feel almost sure that one of these three, early next June—'"

Seeing that Reed was really growing angry, Lefferts hastened to interrupt his host.

"I think you might tell us, Mr. Reed," he said, "what the great beauty of the county looks like?"

"I can't think that this is the time or place for retailing the charms of a young lady as if it were a slave market," answered Reed; and it seemed to Crane that the cook, who had come in to change the plates, looked a little bit disappointed.

"No, not as if it were a slave market," said Lefferts, "because, of course, it isn't."

"I can see no reason, Reed," said Crane, "why you shouldn't give us a hint as to whether Miss Revelly is blond or brunette, tall or short."

"Perhaps I see reasons that you do not, sir," answered the wretched real estate man.

"Well," said Crane, "I tell you what, Jane-Ellen must have seen her often,—Jane-Ellen," he added, "you've seen Miss Revelly. What does she look like?"

Jane-Ellen advanced into the room thoughtfully.

"Well, sir," she said, "it isn't for me to criticize my superiors, nor to say a word against a young lady whom Mr. Reed admires so much, but I have my own reasons, sir, for thinking that there was more in those stories of her engagement than perhaps Mr. Reed himself knows. Servants hear a good deal, you know, sir, and they do say that Miss Revelly—"

"Claudia!" burst from Reed.

"Miss Claudia Revelly, I should say," the cook corrected herself. "Well, sir, as for looks—let me see—she's a tall, commanding looking lady—"

"With flashing black eyes?" asked Crane.

"And masses of blue-black hair."

"A noble brow?"

"A mouth too large for perfect beauty."

"A queenly bearing?"

"An irresistible dignity of manner."

"Jane-Ellen," said Crane, "I feel almost as if Miss Claudia Revelly were standing before me."

"Oh, indeed, sir, if it were she, it's you who would be standing," said the cook.

"For my part," said Crane, turning again to the table, "I had imagined her to myself as quite different. I had supposed her small, soft-eyed, with tiny hands and feet and a mouth—" He was looking at Jane-Ellen's mouth, as if that might give him an inspiration, when Reed interrupted.

"I regret to say, Mr. Crane," he said, "that if this conversation continues to deal disrespectfully with the appearance of a young lady for whom—"

"Disrespectfully!" cried Crane. "I assure you, I had no such intention. I leave it to you, Jane-Ellen, whether anything disrespectful was said about this young lady."

"It did not seem so to me, sir," answered the cook, with all her gentlest manner. "But," she added, glancing humbly at Reed, "of course, it would never do for a servant like me to be setting up my opinion on such a matter against a gentleman like Mr. Reed."

"What I mean is, if Miss Revelly were here, do you think she would object to anything we have said?"

"Indeed, I'm sure she would actually have enjoyed it, sir."

"Well, then, she ought not," shouted Reed sternly.

Jane-Ellen shook her head sadly.

"Ah, sir," she said, "young ladies like Miss Revelly don't always do what they ought to, if report speaks true."

"May I ask, without impertinence, Burton," said Tucker, at this point, "whether it is your intention to give us nothing whatsoever to drink with our dinner?"

"No, certainly not," cried Crane. "Jane-Ellen, why haven't you served the champagne?"

The reason for this omission was presently only too clear. Jane-Ellen had not the faintest idea of how to open the bottle. Crane, listening with one ear to his guests, watched her wrestling with it in a corner, holding it as if it were a venomous reptile.

"For my part," Tucker was saying, "I have a great deal of sympathy with the stand Mr. Reed has taken. Any discussion of a woman behind her back runs at least the risk—"

Suddenly Crane shouted:

"Look out! Don't do that!" He was speaking not to Tucker, but to the cook. His warning, however, came too late. There was the sound of breaking glass and a deep cherry-colored stain dyed the napkin in Jane-Ellen's hand.

All four chairs were pushed back, all four men sprang to her side.

"Let me see your hand."

"Is it badly cut?"

"An artery runs near there."

"Is there any glass in it?"

They crowded around her, nor did any one of them seem to be averse to taking the case entirely into his own control.

"There are antiseptics and bandages upstairs," said Crane.

"Better let me wash it well at the tap in the pantry," urged Reed.

"Does it hurt horribly?" asked Lefferts.

Tucker, putting on his glasses, observed:

"I have had some experience in surgery, and if you will let me examine the wound by a good light—"

"Oh, gentlemen," said Jane-Ellen, "this is absurd. It's nothing but a scratch. Do sit down and finish your dinner, and let me get through my work."

As the injury did not, after a closer observation, seem to be serious, the four men obeyed. But they did so in silence; not even Lefferts and Crane could banter any more. Tucker had never made any pretense of recovering his temper, and Reed seemed to be revolving thoughts of deep import.

As they rose from table, Crane touched the arm of Reed.

"Come into the office, will you? I have something I want to say to you."

"And I to you," said Reed, with feeling.

XII

ONCE in the little office, Crane did not immediately speak. He drew up two chairs, put a log on the fire, turned up the lamp, and in short made it evident that he intended to do that cruel deed sometimes perpetrated by parents, guardians and schoolmasters in interviews of this sort—he was going to leave it to the culprit to make a beginning.

Reed, fidgeting in a nearby chair, did not at once yield to this compulsion, but finally the calm with which Crane was balancing a pen on a pencil broke down his resolution and he said crossly:

"I understood you had something to say to me, Mr. Crane."

Crane threw aside pencil and pen. "I thought it might be the other way," he answered. "But, yes, if you like. I have something to say to you. I have decided to break my lease and leave this house to-morrow."

"You don't mean to go without paying the second instalment of the rent?"

"Why not? The Revellys have broken, or rather have never fulfilled their part of the contract. I took the house on the written understanding that servants were to be supplied, and you are my witness, Mr. Reed, that to-night I have no one left but a cook."

"Oh, come, Mr. Crane! We only agreed to provide the servants. We could not guarantee that you would not dismiss them. You must own they showed no inclination to leave the house."

"No, I'll not deny that," returned Burton grimly.

"No sane man," continued Reed eagerly, "would allow the payment of his rent to depend on whether or not you chose to keep a staff of servants in many ways above the average. You'll not deny, I think, sir, that the cooking has been above the average?"

Crane had reached a state of mind in which it was impossible for him to discuss even the culinary powers of Jane-Ellen, particularly with Reed, and so he slightly shifted the ground.

"Let us," he said, "run over the reasons for which I dismissed them: The housemaid, for calling one of my guests an old harridan; the boy, for habitually smoking my cigarettes, for attempting to strike Mr. Tucker, and finally, for stealing a valuable miniature belonging to the house; the butler, for again introducing this same larcenous boy into the house disguised as a lame old man. The question is not whether I should have kept them, but whether I should not stay on here and have them all arrested."

Reed's face changed. "Oh! I hope you won't do that, Mr. Crane," he said.

Burton saw his advantage. "I should not care," he answered, "to go through life feeling I had been responsible for turning a dangerous gang loose upon the countryside."

"They are not that, sir. I pledge my word they are not that."

"There is a good deal of evidence against that pledge."

"You doubt my word, sir?"

"I feel there is much more to be explained than you seem willing to admit. For instance, how comes it that you are a—I will not say welcome—but at least assured visitor in my kitchen?"

Reed felt himself coloring. "I do not feel called upon," he replied, "to explain my conduct to any one."

"In that case," said Crane, getting to his feet, "this interview might as well end. I shall leave to-morrow, and if you and your friends, the Revellys, feel yourselves aggrieved, we can only take the matter into court. If the record of these servants is as excellent as you seem to think, they can have nothing to fear. If it isn't, the whole matter will be cleared up."

This was the crisis of the conversation, for as Crane moved to the door, Reed stopped him.

"Wait a moment, Mr. Crane," he said. "There are circumstances in this connection that you do not know."

"Yes, I guessed that much."

"If you will sit down, I should like to tell you the whole story."

Crane yielded and sat down, without giving Reed the satisfaction of knowing that his nervousness at the expected revelation was as extreme as Reed's.

"The Revellys, Mr. Crane, are among the most respected of our Southern gentry. They fought for the original liberties of this country, and in the war of secession—"

Crane nodded. "I know my history, Mr. Reed."

"But, sir, their distinguished position and high abilities have not saved them from financial reverses. The grandfather lost everything in the war; and the present owner, Henry Patrick Revelly, has not been completely successful. Last winter a breakdown in his health compelled him to leave the country at short notice. His four children—"

"Four children, Mr. Reed? Two girls and two boys?"

"Four grown children, Mr. Crane. The eldest is twenty-six, the youngest seventeen. They were left with a roof over their heads and a sum of money—a small sum—to provide for them during the absence of their parents. Not a satisfactory arrangement, sir, but made in haste and distress. Mrs. Revelly's devotion to her husband is such that in her alarm for him, she did not perhaps sufficiently consider her children. At the moment when, left alone, their difficulties began to press upon them, your offer, your generous offer, for the house was made. There was no time to submit it to their parents, nor, to be candid with you, would there have been the slightest chance of Mr. Revelly's accepting it. He has never been able to tolerate the mere suggestion of renting Revelly Hall. But the four young people felt differently. It was natural, it was in my opinion commendable, that they decided to move out of their home for the sake of realizing a large sum—the largest sum probably that had come into the family purse for many years. But an obstacle soon appeared. You had insisted that servants should be provided. This was impossible. They tried earnestly. Miss Claudia told me herself that she went everywhere within a radius of twenty miles, except to the jails. At last it became a question of refusing your offer, or of—of—I believe you have already guessed the alternative."

"This is not a time for the exercise of my creative faculties, Mr. Reed. What was their decision?"

Reed's discomfort increased. "I wish you could have been present as I was, Mr. Crane, on that occasion. We were sitting round the fire in the sitting-room, depressed that Miss Claudia's mission had not succeeded, when suddenly she said, with a determination quite at variance with her gentle appearance, 'Well, I've found a cook for him—and a mighty good one, too.' 'Where did you find her?' I asked in astonishment, for only a moment before she had been confessing absolute failure. 'I found her,' she answered, 'where charity begins.' I own that even then I did not get the idea, but her brother Paul, who always understands her, saw at once what was in her mind. 'Yes,' she went on, 'I've found an excellent cook, a good butler, a rather inefficient housemaid, and a dangerous extra boy,' and she looked from one to the other of her family as she spoke. Her meaning was clear. They themselves were to take the places of the servants they could not find. As Paul pointed out, the plan had the advantage of saving them the trouble of finding board and lodgings, elsewhere. Miss Lily was opposed from the start. Her nature, exceedingly refined and retiring, revolted, but no one in the Revelly family can bear up against the combined wills of Paul and Miss Claudia. How the plan was carried out you know."

There was a short silence. It was now some days since Crane had suspected the identity of his servants, an hour since Jane-Ellen had turned at the name of Claudia and made him sure. Nevertheless the certainty that Reed's confession brought was very grateful to him; so grateful that he feared his expression would betray him, and he assumed a look of stern blankness.

Seeing this, Reed thought it necessary to plead the culprits' cause.

"After all, Mr. Crane, was there not courage and self-sacrifice needed? You see this explains everything. The miniature of their grandmother was taken upstairs for fear its likeness to Miss Claudia might betray them. Miss Lily, who as I said never approved of the plan, was constitutionally unable to be calm under the accusation of stealing a hat, made, as I understand, rather roughly by Mrs. Falkener. I should be very sorry if your opinion of the Revelly family—"

"I can't see what my opinion has to do with the situation," said Crane. Every moment now that kept him from Claudia was to him an intolerable bore. He drew his check-book toward him. "However, your story has convinced me of this—my only course is to pay my rent in full."

Reed began to feel the pride of the successful diplomat. "And one other thing, Mr. Crane. You see the necessity of not mentioning this. It would make a great deal of talk in the country. A young lady's name—"

Burton rose quickly. It was not agreeable to him to have Reed pleading with him for the preservation of Claudia's reputation.

"Here's your check," he said.

Reed pressed on. "And another thing will now be equally clear to you, I am sure. Miss Revelly cannot possibly spend the night here alone."

"That," replied Crane, "is a question for Miss Revelly herself to decide. My motors are at her disposal to take her anywhere she may choose to go." And he opened the door as if he expected that Reed would now take his departure.

But Reed did not move. "I cannot go away and leave Miss Revelly here alone with you," he said.

"Of the two alternatives," said Crane, "you might find it more difficult to stay in my house without my consent. But I'll leave it this way—do you think Miss Revelly would regard your presence as a protection?"

"I don't understand you, sir."

"Your last visit to my kitchen did not, I believe, inspire her with confidence. Shall we leave the decision to her?"

Reed went out in silence. He had had no reconciliation with Jane-Ellen since that fatal kiss in the kitchen, and he knew she would not now side with him. He decided to go away and find her brothers.

Lefferts, meanwhile, left alone, had stretched himself on a sofa, and was smoking, with his eyes fixed on the ceiling.

"My dear fellow," cried Crane with some compunction, "were you waiting to see me?"

"I was waiting for my motor," answered the poet. "You know that, imagining this to be an ordinary dinner-party, I ordered it back at a quarter before eleven."

"Where's Tucker?" asked Burton.

At this moment a step was heard on the stairs and Tucker, dressed in a neat gray suit, adapted to traveling, wearing a cap and goggles and carrying his bag, descended the stairs.

On seeing his host he approached and held out his hand. "Good-by, Burton," he said, "I hope the time will come when you will forgive me for having tried too hard to serve you. For myself, I entirely forgive your hasty rudeness. I hope we part friends."

Crane hesitated, and then shook hands with his lawyer. "There's no use in pretending, Tucker," he said, "that I feel exactly friendly to you, and, if you'll forgive my saying so, I can't believe that you feel so to me. You and I have got on each other's nerves lately; and that's the truth. How much that means, only time can show. Sometimes it is very important, sometimes very trivial; but while such a state exists, I agree with you that two people are better apart. Good-by."

Here, Jane-Ellen, who had just finished putting the dining-room in order, came out into the hall followed by Willoughby. As she saw Tucker, she had one of her evil inspirations.

Springing forward, she exclaimed: "Oh, wasn't it a pity, sir, you had to do your own packing! Let me put your bag in the motor for you."

Tucker was again caught by one of his moments of indecision. He did not want Jane-Ellen to carry his luggage, but he did not consider it dignified to wrestle with her for the possession of it, so that in the twinkling of an eye she had seized it and carried it down the steps.

But he was not utterly without resource. He had been holding a two-dollar bill in his hand, more from recollections of other visits than because he now expected to find any one left to fee. This, as Jane-Ellen came up the steps, he thrust into her hand, saying clearly:

"Thank you, my girl, there's for your trouble."

Jane-Ellen just glanced at it, and then crumpling it into a ball she threw it across the hall. Willoughby, who like many other sheltered creatures retained his playfulness late in life, bounded after it, caught it up in his paws, threw it about, and finally set on it with his sharp little teeth and bit it to pieces. But neither Tucker nor the cook waited to see the end. He got into the car and rolled away, and she went back to the kitchen.

Crane glanced at Lefferts, to whom plainly his duty as host pointed, and then he hurried down the kitchen stairs, closing the door carefully behind him.

XIII

JANE-ELLEN was shaking out her last dishcloth, her head turned well over her shoulder to avoid the shower of spray that came from it. He seated himself on the kitchen-table, and watched her for some time in silence.

"And is that the way you treat all presents, Jane-Ellen," he asked, "throwing them to Willoughby to tear to pieces?"

"That was not a present, sir. Presents are between equals, I've always thought."

"Then, Jane-Ellen, I don't see how you can ever hope to get any."

She looked at him and smiled. "Your talk is too deep and clever for a poor girl like me to understand, sir."

He smiled back. "They've all gone, Jane-Ellen," he said.

The news did not seem to disturb the cook in the least. Reed would have been shocked by the calmness with which she received it.

"And now you're all alone, sir," she replied.

"Absolutely alone."

She was still pattering about the kitchen, putting the last things to rights, but—or so it seemed to Crane—a little busier than her occupation warranted.

"They left early, sir, didn't they? But then it did not seem to me that they were really enjoying themselves, not even Mr. Lefferts, though he is such an amusing gentleman. Every one seemed sad, sir, except you."

"I was sad, too, Jane-Ellen."

"Indeed, sir?"

"Something was said at dinner that distressed me deeply."

"By whom, sir?"

"By you."

She did not stop her work nor seem very much surprised, but of course she asked what her unfortunate speech had been.

"I was sorry to hear you say you believed in Miss Revelly's triple engagement."

At this she did stop short, and immediately in his vicinity. "But I did not know you knew Miss Revelly."

"Yet I do."

"And when I was describing her—"

"It was as if I saw her before me."

"I am sorry I said anything about a friend of yours, sir. I had supposed she was quite a stranger to you."

"Sometimes it seems to me, too, as if she were a stranger," Crane answered. "Each time I see her, Jane-Ellen, she seems to me so lovely and wonderful and miraculous that it is as if I saw her for the first time. Sometimes when I am away from her it seems to me quite ridiculous to believe that such a creature exists in this rather tiresome old world, and I feel like rushing back from wherever I am to assure myself that she isn't just a creation of my own passionate desire. In this sense, I think she will always be a stranger, always be a surprise to me even if I should have the great felicity of spending the rest of my days with her. Does it bore you, Jane-Ellen, to hear me talking this way about my own feelings?"

Jane-Ellen did not answer; indeed something seemed to suggest that she could not speak, but she shook her head and Burton went on.

"So you see why it distressed me to hear from so good an authority as yourself that she had already engaged herself three times. It is not that I am of a jealous nature, Jane-Ellen, but when I ask her to be my wife, if she should say yes, I should want to feel sure that that meant—"

"Oh, Mr. Crane!" said Jane-Ellen, "I said that to make Mr. Reed angry."

"And there was no truth in it?"

There was a pause. Jane-Ellen looked down and wriggled her shoulders a little.

"Well," she admitted, "there was some truth in it. They were not exactly engagements. We think in this part of the world that there's something almost too harsh in a flat no—oh! the truth is," she added, suddenly changing her tone, "that girls don't know what they're doing until they find that they have fallen in love themselves."

"And do you think by any chance that this revelation may have come to Miss Revelly?"

"I know right well it has," answered Jane-Ellen.

"Oh, my dear love!" cried Crane and took her into his arms.

The kitchen clock, loudly ticking, looked down upon them on one side, and Willoughby, loudly purring, looked up at them from the other, and a good deal of ticking and purring was done before Claudia broke the silence by saying, like one to whom a good idea has come rather late:

"But I never said it was through you that the revelation came."

"You mustn't say that it hasn't even in fun—not yet."

"When may I?"

"When we've been married five years."

Sometime later, when, that is to say, they had talked a little longer in the kitchen, and then shut it up for the night, and had gone and sat a little while in the parlor so that he might realize that she really was Miss Claudia Revelly, and they had sat a little while in the office so that she might act out for him the impression he had made an her during that first famous interview when he had reproved her conduct, when all these important conversations had taken place, Crane at last took her hand and said gravely: "I mustn't keep you up any longer. Good night, my darling." And he added, after an instant, "I'm so glad—so grateful—that your mind doesn't work like Reed's and Tucker's."

"Like theirs—in what way?"

"I'm glad you haven't thought it necessary to make any protest at our being here alone."

A slight motion of his beloved's shoulders told him she was not fully at one with him.

"How foolish, Burton, of course I trust you absolutely, only—"

"Only what—"

She evidently felt that it was a moment when something decisive must be done, for she came and laid her head, not on his shoulder, but as near as she could reach, which was about in the turn of his elbow.

His arm was coldly limp. "Only what?" he repeated.

"Only we're not really alone."

"What do you mean, Claudia?"

"They're all here—my brothers and sister."

"What, Smithfield, and Lily, and even Brindlebury?"

She nodded in as much space as she had.

"Where are they?" he asked.

"They're playing Coon-Can in the garret. And oh," she added with a sudden spasm of recollection, "they'll be so hungry! They haven't had anything to eat for ages. I promised to bring them something as soon as the house was quiet, only you put everything out of my head."

"We'll give them a party in the dining-room—our first," said Crane. "I'll write the invitation, and we'll send Lefferts to the garret with it."

"Don't you think I'd better go up and explain?" said Claudia.

"The invitation will explain," answered Burton. It read: "Mr. Burton Crane and Miss Claudia Revelly request the pleasure of the Revellys' company at supper immediately."

They roused Lefferts, who had by this time fallen into a comfortable sleep. "Just run up and give this note to the people you'll find in the garret, there's a good fellow," said Crane.

Lefferts sat up, rubbing his eyes. "The people I'll find in the garret," he murmured. "But how about the little black men in the chimney, and the ghosts who live in the wall? This is the strangest house, Crane, the very strangest house I ever knew." But he took the note and wandered slowly upstairs with it, shaking his head.

On the landing of the second story, his eye caught the whisk of a skirt, and pursuing it instantly, he came upon Lily. He cornered her in the angle of the stairs.

"Hold on," he said, "I have a note for you, at least I have if you are one of the people who live in the garret."

Lily, knowing nothing of the explanation that had taken place between Reed and Crane, was not a little alarmed at being thus caught in a house from which she had been so recently dismissed. She did not think quickly in a crisis, and now she could find nothing to say but "I don't exactly live in the garret."

"How interesting it would be," observed Lefferts, "if you would sit down here on the stairs and tell me who you are."

"There's nothing to tell," said Lily, wondering what she had better admit. "I'm just the housemaid."

"Oh," cried Lefferts, "then there are lots of things to tell. I have always wanted to ask housemaids a number of questions. For instance, why is it that you always drop the broom with which you sweep the stairs at six in the morning? Why do you fancy it will conduce to any one's comfort to shut the blinds and turn on all the lights in a bedroom on a hot summer evening? Why do you hide the pillows and extra covering so that one never finds them until one is packing to go away the next morning? If you are a housemaid, you do these things; and if you do these things, you must know why you do them."

Lily smiled. "I'm afraid I was a very poor housemaid," she answered. "Anyhow, I'm not even that any more. I was dismissed."

"Indeed," said Lefferts. "Now that must be an interesting experience. I have had several perfectly good businesses drop from under me, but I have never been dismissed. Might I ask what led to it in your case?"

A reminiscent smile stole over Lily's face. "Mr. Crane dismissed me," she said, "for saying something which I believe he thought himself. I called Mrs. Falkener an old harridan."

Lefferts shouted with pleasure.

"If Crane had had a spark of intellectual honesty, he'd have raised your wages," he said. "It's just what he wanted to say himself."

"Oh! I was glad to be dismissed," returned she. "I never approved of the whole plan anyhow." And then fearing she had betrayed too much, she added, "And now you might tell me who you are."

"My name is Lefferts."

"Any relation to the poet?"

It would be impossible to deny that this unexpected proof of his fame was agreeable to Lefferts. The conversation on the stairs became more absorbing, and the note was less likely to be delivered at all.

In the meantime Claudia, while setting the table in the dining-room, had sent Crane down to the kitchen floor to get something out of the ice-box. As Crane approached this object about which so many sentimental recollections gathered, he saw he had been anticipated. A figure was already busy extracting from it a well-filled plate. At his step, the figure turned quickly. It was Brindlebury.

Even Brindlebury seemed to appreciate that, after all that had occurred in connection with his last departure, to be caught once again in Crane's house was a serious matter. It would have been easy enough to save himself by a confession that he was one of the Revellys, but to tell this without the consent of his brother and sisters would have been considered traitorous in the extreme.

He backed away from the ice-box. "Mr. Crane," he said, with unusual seriousness, "you probably feel that an explanation is due you." And there he stopped, not being able at the moment to think of anything to say.

Crane took pity on him. "Brindlebury," he said, "it would be ungenerous of me to conceal from you that our relative positions are reversed. At the present moment the power is all in your hands. Have a cigarette. I believe you used to like this brand."

"Only when I had smoked all my own."

"You see, Brindlebury, it is not only that I am obliged to forgive you, I have to go further. I have to make up to you. For the truth is, Brindlebury, that I want to marry your sister."

"You want to marry Jane-Ellen?"

"More than I can tell you."

"And what does she say?"

"She likes the idea."

"Bless my soul! you are going to be my brother-in-law."

"No rose without its thorn, I understand."

The situation was too tempting to the boy's love of a joke. He seated himself on the top of the ice-box and folded his arms.

"I do not know," he said, "that I should be justified in giving my consent to any such marriage. Would it tend to make my sister happy? The woman who marries above her social position—the man who marries his cook—is bound to regret it. Have you considered, Mr. Crane, that however you may value my sister yourself, many of your proud friends would not receive her?"

"To my mind, Brindlebury, these social distinctions are very unimportant. Even you I should be willing to have to dinner now and then when we were alone."

"The deuce you would," said Brindlebury, and added, "but suppose my sister's lack of refinement—"

"I can't let you talk like that even in fun, Revelly," said Crane. "Get off your ice-box and let us go back to Claudia."

"Ah, you knew all along?"

"I have suspected for some time. Reed told me this evening."

But when they reached the dining-room, Claudia was not there. She had gone herself to tell her news to her brother Paul. He was sitting alone in the garret with the remnants of the game of Coon-Can before him. Claudia came and put her hand on his shoulder, but he did not move.

"Do you know what I have made up my mind to do?" he said. "I mean to go and make a clean breast of this to Crane. The game is about up, and I don't think he's had a square deal. He's a nice fellow, and I'd like to put myself straight with him."

Claudia remained standing behind her brother, as she asked, "You like him, Paul?"

"Very much indeed. I think he's behaved mighty well through all this. Don't you like him?"

There was an instant's pause, and then Claudia answered simply:

"I love him, Paul."

Her brother sprang to his feet. "Don't say that even to yourself, my dear," he said. "You don't know what men of his sort are like. Spoilt, run after, cold-blooded. He's not like the men you've ruled over all your life—"

"No, indeed, he's not," said Claudia.

"My dear girl," her brother went on seriously, "this is not like you. You must put this out of your head. After all, that oughtn't to be very hard. You've hardly known the man more than a few days."

"Paul, that shows you don't know what love is. It hasn't anything to do with time, or your own will. It's just there in an instant. People talk as if it were common, as if every one fell in love, but I don't believe they do—not like this. Look at me. I've only known this man as you say a little while, I've only talked to him a few times, and some of those were disagreeable, and yet the idea of spending my life with him not only seems natural, but all the rest of my life—you and my home—seem strange and unfamiliar. I feel the way you do when you've been living abroad hearing strange languages and suddenly some one speaks to you in your own native tongue. When Burton—"

"Burton?"

"Didn't I tell you we're engaged?"

"My dear Claudia, you must admit we don't really know anything about him."

"You have the rest of your life for finding out, Paul."

They went downstairs presently to supper—a meal that promised to be a good deal more agreeable than dinner had been. For all

Paul's expressed doubts, he had every disposition to make himself pleasant to his future brother-in-law, and even Lily had felt his charm. Lefferts, the only person in the dark as to the whole situation, served as an excellent audience. All four recounted—together and in turn—the whole story, from the moment when the idea had first occurred to Claudia, at eleven years of age, that she would like to learn to cook, down to the subtlest allusion of that evening's dinner-table.

Then suddenly there was a loud peal at the front door-bell. Every one knew instantly what it was—Reed returning to make one more effort to save Claudia's reputation.

"Well," said Paul, sinking down in his chair and thrusting his hands still deeper into his pockets, "I shan't let him in. My future depends on my getting over the habit of answering bells."

"Same here," said Brindlebury.

"I certainly shan't open the door for the man," said Crane, "and Claudia shall go only over my dead body."

Again the bell rang.

Lily rose. "I shall let him in," she said, "I think you are all very unjust to Randolph."

Claudia smiled as her sister left the room.

"There," she said, "that's all right. No one has such a good effect on Randolph as Lily has. In fifteen minutes he will be perfectly calm and polite. In half an hour she will have persuaded him he likes things better the way they are."

"I should think," said Lefferts, glancing at Claudia, "that it might take her a little longer than that."

It did take her a little longer.

THE END

Lightning Source UK Ltd.
Milton Keynes UK
UKHW041848090223
416678UK00005B/217/J